Under the golde
they made love

"I should be working," Liz murmured as they sat, still naked, at the edge of the pool dangling their legs in the water, sipping the chilled champagne and eating the sweet, juicy flesh of a nectarine.

"On Monday we'll do that. For now, let's concentrate on life's other pleasures. With luck we'll be able to paint in our old age, but we may not be able to spend our afternoons doing this...." David nodded in the direction of the sun mattresses.

"They say people can make love all their lives." Liz said idly, watching the gleaming golden reflections in the pool.

"I hope so," he said dryly.

Finally, Liz thought, it was her turn to feel happy again. But could this sun-filled, carefree Mediterranean life really go on forever?

ANNE WEALE is one of Harlequin's busiest writers—and also one of the most traveled. She gave up her original career as a journalist to follow her husband to the Far East. British citizens by birth, Anne and her husband have lived for the past five years in a Spanish villa high above the Mediterranean. They have traveled extensively researching new romantic backgrounds—New England, Florida, the Caribbean, Italy and their latest journeys have taken them through Canada to Australia and the Pacific. Swimming, interior decorating, antique hunting and needlepoint are among Anne's many interests.

Books by Anne Weale

HARLEQUIN PRESENTS
504—PASSAGE TO PAXOS
511—A TOUCH OF THE DEVIL
541—PORTRAIT OF BETHANY
565—WEDDING OF THE YEAR
613—ALL THAT HEAVEN ALLOWS
622—YESTERDAY'S ISLAND
670—ECSTASY
846—FRANGIPANI

HARLEQUIN ROMANCE
1512—THAT MAN SIMON
1629—A TREASURE FOR LIFE
1747—THE FIELDS OF HEAVEN
1848—LORD OF THE SIERRAS
2411—THE LAST NIGHT AT PARADISE
2436—RAIN OF DIAMONDS
2484—BED OF ROSES

Don't miss any of our special offers. Write to us at the following address for information on our newest releases.

Harlequin Reader Service
901 Fuhrmann Blvd., P.O. Box 1397, Buffalo, NY 14240
Canadian address: P.O. Box 603,
Fort Erie, Ont. L2A 5X3

ANNE WEALE

girl in a golden bed

Harlequin Books

TORONTO • NEW YORK • LONDON
AMSTERDAM • PARIS • SYDNEY • HAMBURG
STOCKHOLM • ATHENS • TOKYO • MILAN

Harlequin Presents first edition September 1987
ISBN 0-373-11013-8

Original hardcover edition published in 1986
by Mills & Boon Limited

CHAPTER ONE

Liz had been restless all day, unable to work well and equally unable to relax and be pleasurably idle.

She knew why she had the fidgets. She was lonely for someone to talk to; more than that, for someone to love. Twice in her life—once when she was very young—she had given her heart to a man, only to find that what she had hoped was true love was in fact a counterfeit.

Those experiences had left her afraid to love again in case she made another mistake. She was no longer a young girl. She was twenty-eight. A true disciple of Germaine Greer and Gloria Steinem, two feminists whom she admired, but whose precepts she couldn't quite bring herself to follow, would have gone down the hill and sat in one of Portofino's waterfront cafés on her own, and not felt lonely. Or she would have picked a man out and gone to bed with him.

But much as she longed to have a loving companion to share her bed at the Villa Delphini, Liz had always shunned trivial sex. Even after six months of loneliness since the painful end of her partnership with Richard, she wasn't tempted to try a casual relationship.

There was junk food and there was junk sex, and she didn't care for either. She wanted the best of everything life had to offer, which, between a man and a woman, meant a deeply committed, caring, loving relationship. If she couldn't have the best, she preferred to go without—for ever, if necessary. When she gave her heart for the third time—perhaps *if* was the operative word—that's the way it would be ... for ever.

But sometimes, and this warm Italian summer night was one of them, it was hard to repress the longing to be what a poet had called, 'happy on a tousled bed'.

There were many women of her age who had been married for years and had one or two children. Liz was conscious of what she was missing. Perhaps those young wives and mothers, at times overburdened with their responsibilities, envied women like herself their freedom and independence. But at least they never experienced the aching loneliness which was making her miserable tonight.

The bed in the room she had chosen when she took possession of the villa during its owner's long absence was at least two centuries old. Its canopy was supported by ornately carved and gilded columns round which flying cherubs, called *amorini*, wound garlands of flowers. On the underside of the canopy was a mirror, dimmed and flecked by time.

Lying in bed, her hair fanning over the pillow, Liz could look up and see a misty image of her long-legged slender figure in the antique mirror overhead; a mirror put there, she knew, to heighten the pleasure of the men and women who had not slept alone in the huge bed.

As she visualised the many couples whose embraces the mirror had reflected, her own longing for love grew more urgent; a burning need to feel strong arms around her and a man's warm demanding mouth on hers.

Most of the time her painting absorbed and fulfilled her. She was an artist first and a woman second; or so she had always told herself. It was because Richard had never understood that, and because his unreasonable demands on her time had begun to drain her creative energy that, in the end, she had been forced to leave him. It had been an act of self-preservation.

She didn't regret that decision. Here, in this romantic house perched on a steep wooded hillside overlooking one of the most picturesque ports in the Mediterranean, she had been content with her solitude.

Until today.

All today she had been consumed by loneliness; a deep-seated need to talk, to share, to respond, that refused to be ignored.

Sleeping pills were not part of her lifestyle. She had never needed them. But tonight, if she had possessed a pill which would knock her out, she would have taken it rather than lie awake, racked by a futile longing for a tender, passionate, sensitive, considerate man who probably didn't exist except in her daydreams.

While Liz Redwood was wrestling with sleeplessness, on the other side of Europe at Schiphol Airport, Amsterdam, a tall lean man with fair hair and arrestingly vivid blue eyes was boarding a delayed flight to Genoa.

He was on the last lap of a journey which had taken him around the world and lasted for more than two years. At the start he had felt he would probably never return to the house above Portofino which held many poignant memories for him.

Now he was tired of journeying, tired of living in hotels and rented apartments. Time had dulled the despair which had driven him out of Italy. Weary of being a nomad, forever unpacking and repacking, he wanted to settle down and stay put for a while. As the only logical place to do that was at the Villa Delphini, he had decided to go back.

Knowing his Italian housekeeper had kept the place aired and ready for occupation whenever he chose to reappear, he hadn't cabled to warn her he was on his way home. He was fond of old Anna, and valued her services, but he didn't want her waiting to welcome him with a flood of excited questions about his travels and how long he meant to remain in Portofino.

That was something he didn't know, and wouldn't until he had walked through the silent rooms and discovered if they were still haunted.

He had been considerably jet-lagged before the delay at Schiphol. By the time he reached his destination, he was too tired to think of anything but stretching himself at full length on a well-sprung mattress and sleeping the clock round.

It was with passing surprise that, on entering his bedroom, he noticed Anna had neglected to close all the shutters. Not that it mattered in summer, but it wasn't like her to be careless about leaving the villa securely locked and barred against intruders.

Dumping his flight bag on the floor—he had left all his other luggage downstairs in the hall—he began to take off the clothes he had put on in Canada.

Stripped, his tall broad-shouldered frame still carrying more muscle than flesh, although he was now in his forties, he debated taking a shower, but decided it could wait until he woke up.

Right now he was totally bushed. All he needed was sleep, and more sleep. Yawning, dazed with fatigue, he turned to the dais where the giant bed offered unlimited space for his aircraft-cramped legs.

On that side of the large, lofty room the shutters were closed. The gilded pillars glinted mysteriously in the shadows. He had thought he might have to fetch sheets from the herb-scented linen room. But the bed was already made up. Too exhausted to find this surprising, he lay down and drew up the top sheet to cover his waist. Within seconds he was unconscious.

Outside, on the thickly wooded hillside, the twitter of birdsong grew stronger. The sleeping man stirred and turned over, his hand coming into contact with the once-familiar smooth curve of a feminine hip.

Half woken by the dawn chorus, he moved his hand up to a slim waist, edging his body closer, his hand sliding further round in quest of a soft warm globe to fill his palm as it had in the past, before his long self-imposed exile, before the days of laughter and nights of love had come to an abrupt end.

Within the circle of his arm, Liz gave a faint drowsy murmur as her back felt the solid warmth of a masculine chest and the long legs close behind hers.

Still deeply submerged in the heavy, exhausted slumber which follows hours of restlessness, she began to dream Richard was holding her. They were on board his yacht, on holiday at Puerto de la Duquesa, still happy together, still a pair.

For a few seconds, in her dream, she relived the time when her future had seemed safe and settled; it being just a matter of time before they would marry and find a place in the country where children could grow up in fresh air and she could keep cats and dogs and even a hive of bees and a donkey with neat black hooves.

Then the gentle fondling of her body through the cool, flimsy lawn of her nightdress brought her floating rapidly upwards through the levels of consciousness. One moment she was relaxed. The next instant she was awake, beginning to realise something was wrong—but what? Seconds later she was tensing with shock and alarm at the realisation that the hand on her breast was no figment of her subconscious, but a living flesh and blood hand which had no right to be touching her.

As her heart began to beat with frightened thumps, the hand was removed, there was a violent movement in the bed behind her and a voice exclaimed, 'What the hell . . .?'

Jerking into a sitting position and peering through the gloom of first light, Liz realised she was in bed with a man she had never seen before.

Before she could react to this appalling discovery, he snapped on the far-side reading light, revealing himself as a very large, naked man—though the sheet covered him to the waist—with tousled fair hair and a noticeably unshaven jaw. The stubble glinted in the lamplight.

In the normal way, Liz was a self-possessed person who could cope with most situations. But not with this one.

After instinctively snatching the edge of the sheet and holding it high against her chest, she gaped at him with her mouth open, not knowing what to do or say.

'Who the devil are you?' he demanded abruptly, as if she, not he, was the one with no right to be there.

In a high nervous squeak, quite unlike her normal rather low-pitched speaking voice, she said, 'Who are *you*? H-how did you get in?' The unsteadiness of the second question betrayed her continued alarm.

Even though, in spite of the stubble, he didn't look an unpleasant character, she was sharply conscious of her vulnerability, alone in an isolated house, if he turned nasty.

He said, 'With my key. This is my house.'

Her large, long-lashed amber eyes widened. This wasn't how, from Anna's description of him, she had visualised Sir David Castle, the English baronet who owned the Villa Delphini. The Italian had made him sound a much older man; possibly, judging by her pursed lips when Liz had enquired about his marital status, a homosexual. In fact he looked about ten years older than Liz and not in the least effeminate. Anything but.

While she was gathering her wits from this second shock he said, 'You'd better look the other way. I'm going to put something on.'

Before she could avert her eyes, he flung back the sheet and swung long brown legs over the edge of the bed. A lithe upward movement brought him to his feet and he stepped off the dais surrounding the bed and crossed the dark marble floor in the direction of the adjoining bathroom.

Without intending to watch him, Liz found her artist's eye riveted by a pair of broad shoulders and a powerful, muscular back which narrowed to lean hips. He was at least six feet tall, probably more, and the only part of his finely proportioned body which wasn't deeply tanned was a small wedge-shaped area of his backside. Even that wasn't white, but merely a paler shade of gold.

As soon as he had disappeared, she sprang out of bed and reached for her ruffled and beribboned white eyelet peignoir. Most of her day clothes were simple, classic, understated. But she adored pretty ultra-feminine underwear and night clothes, even when there was no one but herself to see them.

She was fastening the sash of the robe when Sir David reappeared, a large bath towel wrapped round his hips.

'My bathrobe isn't there now. This will have to do for the moment.'

Even though her filmy nightdress was now modestly concealed, Liz found it hard to meet his gaze with composure when only a few minutes earlier she had woken to find him touching her as intimately as a lover.

She concluded that he must have thought, as she had, that he was in bed with someone he knew, or had known.

It was years since she had experienced one of the distressingly vivid blushes which had afflicted her as a teenager. But the gleam of sardonic amusement at the contretemps in which they found themselves which she recognised in his blue eyes made a bright blush burn her face and throat.

'How did you manage to persuade Anna to allow you the run of the place?' he asked.

'I didn't persuade her. She persuaded me. I was living down there in the village.' Liz gestured towards the windows overlooking the sea and the little port. 'She said it would be quieter up here, and that you often let the villa when you were away for a long time. Isn't that true?'

'No, it isn't,' he told her drily. 'But it may be that Anna has been letting it without my knowledge. What rent are you paying her?'

She told him.

Sir David raised an eyebrow. 'Didn't that strike you as suspiciously cheap for a villa of this size?'

'Yes, it did, and I queried it with her. She said it wouldn't be fair to charge me the full rent a family would pay. I've only been using this room and the kitchen. All the others are locked up, except when Anna is dusting them. I have all my meals outside on the terrace. She gave me the impression you would prefer a low rent than no rent at all. She said most of the people who come here prefer to stay at the Hotel Splendido where they can mix with other visitors. You can hardly blame me for taking your housekeeper at her word, Sir David. I don't think I'm unduly gullible. It seemed to me more than likely that a villa like this, with its old-world grandeur, wouldn't appeal to the kind of people who have money now.'

As she spoke, she remembered Richard and his preference for flashy luxury rather than the discreet form. The slightly shabby *grand luxe* of the past, which had always appealed to her and which the Villa epitomised, would not have pleased him. He would never have rented a house which lacked stereo, TV and video, microwave and all the other gadgets he considered essential to his comfort.

A slight frown contracted the brows of the man on the other side of the bed.

He said, 'I prefer to be known as Mr Castle.' The frown vanished and the glint of humour returned. 'However, in the circumstances, why not call me David? What's your name?'

'Liz . . . Liz Redwood.'

'Are you alone here, Liz?'

Had he asked her that before she knew who he was, she would have pretended she had a brother sleeping in another room. Now she felt safe in telling the truth.

'Yes, I am.'

'You must be a very sound sleeper not to have heard me come in. I didn't notice you because I was out on my feet—I'd been travelling for thirty-six hours. I fell into bed, asleep when I hit the pillow.' He paused for a moment, looking thoughtfully at her. 'When I began to wake up and knew I wasn't alone, I mistook you for somebody else.'

She thought that was all he was going to say until, unexpectedly, he added, 'Someone who used to live here . . . a long time ago.'

This rider made Liz realise that what she had taken for Anna's tight-lipped disapproval of homosexual propensities might have been censure of another nature. Perhaps the woman he mentioned had been his mistress. Anna, who undoubtedly had been a virgin when she married and had worn black throughout the twenty years of her widowhood, would have disapproved of that relationship almost as much as if his companion had been a man.

While they had been talking the room had been growing lighter. Always an early riser and now wide awake, Liz said, 'It will take me some time to clear my things out of your room. If you're worn out from travelling, I think the best plan would be for me to make up a bed for you in one of the other rooms. Then you can catch up your sleep and, by the time you wake up, I'll be packed and ready to move out.'

Instead of agreeing to her suggestion, he said, 'How long have you been living here, and when does your tenancy end?'

'I've been here for two months. I was going to stay here all summer. But I can easily find somewhere else to live.'

'I doubt that. It's high season now. Whatever Anna may have told you, the fact is that Portofino is a very popular resort. Without an advance reservation, accommodation is hard to find, and expensive. Anyway, I have no objection to your staying here. There's plenty of room for the two of us.'

'I couldn't do that,' she protested. 'It's kind of you to suggest it, but I couldn't stay on now you're back. You want your house to yourself—as I should, if I were you.'

'Why don't we discuss it over breakfast? I'll catch up some sleep later on. At the moment I feel like some coffee and something to eat. The food on my flight from Canada wasn't bad as airline food goes, but they served it at times when I wasn't hungry. Now I am. Can you fix me some breakfast while I have a quick shower?'

Liz had a talent for cooking which, but for her superior talent with a paintbrush, she might have turned into a career. But, following the break with Richard, she had made a vow never to be coerced into taking on any domestic chores simply because she was a woman and therefore by tradition the one to organise meals and other household arrangements.

The over-indulged son of a doting mother, Richard had been incapable of cooking anything more complicated than a hard-boiled egg, and moreover had had no intention of applying his considerable gifts to what he regarded as women's work.

That Liz was a professional artist whose exquisitely detailed paintings, none larger in size than a paperback, were snapped up by eager buyers in Europe and North America, had not made him take her career as seriously as his own.

At first he had kept this attitude under hatches. Only gradually had it emerged that he thought a woman's primary function was to serve a man's comfort and pleasure. If she could run a career at the same time, so much the better. As long as it didn't conflict with the career of the man in her life.

It was on the tip of her tongue to point out to David Castle that she also liked to shower when she got up. If he wanted a cooked breakfast he would have to prepare it himself. She ate only fruit and yoghurt first thing in the morning.

However, on second thoughts, it seemed ungracious to refuse to fix breakfast for a man who had made a long flight and was probably jet-lagged, even though the cornea surrounding those amazing cornflower-blue irises didn't show any red veining, nor were his eyelids puffy. Maybe he wasn't a drinker. That helped to cut down jet-lag and, with that flat hard midriff and clearly defined jawline, he had to be a man of fairly abstemious habits.

'With pleasure. What would you like?' she said, in answer to his question.

'Whatever you can rustle up. You'll want a shower, too, no doubt. I'll use one of the other bathrooms.'

He turned away and went to gather up some clothes flung carelessly over the seat of a Renaissance chair. Then, his garments collected, he picked up a flight bag of serviceable olive green nylon with tan leather reinforcements. It looked weighty—perhaps with books—and his upper arm bulged for a moment as he hoisted it on to his shoulder.

Without glancing at her again, he left the room. She knew he would have no problem entering another bedroom. Although, as she had remarked, the other rooms were kept locked when Anna was not attending to them, the housekeeper never removed the keys from the latches. She had explained this by saying that, if someone broke in, it was better for moveable objects to be stolen than for the tall, handsome doors to be opened by force and damaged.

Left alone, Liz went to the bathroom and brushed the excellent teeth she had inherited genetically from her American mother. Then she washed her face with a special soap discovered on her first trip to New York. She had a fine, rather dry complexion which she was careful never to expose to sunlight without first applying a high-protection cream.

As she smoothed lather over her forehead and down the straight bridge of her nose, she found herself thinking that if David Castle had kissed her awake his stubble would have rasped her skin. She had never been kissed by a man of his almost Scandinavian fairness and she would have expected his early morning chin to be considerably less bristly than that of the Italians with their pronounced dark beard shadow.

The only two men in her life had been dark-haired Anglo-Saxons. Until today she had thought she preferred them to Nordic types. Blue eyes had always seemed cold to her. But there was nothing cold about this man's eyes.

She had shed her robe before washing. Now she grasped the loose folds of her nightie and pulled it over her head. The mirror behind the wide rose-marble washbasin, where the water came out of the snarling jaws of a lion's mask, reflected a still girlish figure with small high breasts, a neat waist and hips and thighs which looked good in pants and shorts.

Fortunately—now why did she think that?—it was only a few days since she had coloured her hair, changing its natural mouse brown to a more interesting strawberry blonde, as she did every three or four weeks.

Twisting it into a thick skein, she bundled it into a cap and stepped inside the modern glass-panelled shower cabinet built in one corner of the large room. There was also a huge marble bath, shaped like a sarcophagus, but she had never used it.

Turning the shower full on, she closed her eyes as the water began to beat down on her and wondered if it would be difficult to find alternative accommodation. She wished she didn't have to leave. She had come to love the Villa Delphini.

Normally she had breakfast in a semi-transparent *pareu* which Richard had bought for her in one of the expensive boutiques at Puerto Bañus, another marina development on the Spanish Costa del Sol where he liked to spend most of his holidays.

It had been an unusually generous gesture on his

part; prompted, she had realised unhappily, by a wish to make a favourable impression on the husband of the couple they were with, rather than a desire to please Liz.

Having a good income of her own, she had never wanted him to spend a lot of money on her. But she would have liked it if, sometimes, he had bought an inexpensive gift which showed some insight into her character and tastes. In the early stages of their affair, it had delighted her to hunt for presents for him. Richard had never reciprocated. The presents he had given her had all been things which required no effort on his part: flowers, scent, chocolates, current best-sellers, not even lovingly inscribed.

Now, looking back on the three years they'd spent together, she was amazed it had taken her so long to fall out of love with him. She could forgive her first love affair. At eighteen she had been too young to recognise a physical infatuation for what it was. To repeat the mistake at twenty-four could not be excused as youthful folly. She should have known better: seen Richard Fox for what *he* was.

A completely self-centred egoist with tacky values who had never, not even at the beginning, intended to marry her. How could she not have seen through all his specious reasons for postponing total commitment? How could she have been such a fool?

Yet now, seeing him in his true colours, she could only be glad they had never been husband and wife or, horrifying thought, parents. Herself the child of a broken marriage, Liz hated to think she might have inflicted that condition on other children—her children.

This morning, instead of the gauzy *pareu*, she put on a natural linen top and a deeper beige drawstring skirt with slit pockets in the side seams. Normally, around the villa her only other garment would have been cotton micro-briefs. Today, with a man in the house, she put on a bra—only two wisps of net joined by narrow ribbons, but a bra.

He was in the kitchen before her, using the liquidiser to make fruit juice. A large tray was already stacked with china and silver to carry out to the terrace.

Switching off the machine, he said, 'Let's start again from now, shall we?'

As he crossed the big kitchen towards her, she took in the dark honey colour of his neatly combed, shower-wet hair, and the fact that he looked slightly older when it wasn't rumpled. No, perhaps not older, just smoother, more the debonair aristocrat which, for some reason, he preferred not to be known as.

When he reached her, as if it were their first meeting, he held out his hand, saying, 'How do you do, Miss Redwood. I'm David Castle. I'm sorry you've had no notice of my homecoming, but it needn't incommode you. I may only stay a short time. I hope you've been comfortable during your time at the villa?'

His manner was so much that of a well-bred man introducing himself to a paying guest that she could almost believe they had never met before. If they hadn't, would she have felt this same tremor as his long hand folded round hers?

'Very comfortable, thank you. It's the most beautiful house I've ever stayed in.'

Although she was wearing black cotton espadrilles with black tapes criss-crossed round her ankles and rope-covered wedges adding two inches to her barefoot height of five feet six, he was still much the taller.

Keeping hold of her hand, he looked searchingly down at her, making her glad she had taken the time to pencil a black line under the rim of her upper eyelids to give subtle emphasis to her naturally long dark lashes, and to rub a gloss-stick over her lips.

Her hair was now brushed and confined in a long thick plait, starting from high on her crown. Loose hair was too hot in this climate and the plait could be pinned up easily when she wanted to swim in the pool on the lower terrace.

The one snag with her present hair colour was that both the sun and the chemicals in the pool tended to make it turn brassy. For that reason, and also to shade her eyes when she was working outside, she seldom went out without a straw hat on her head; a man's hat which she thought more chic than the styles designed for female tourists.

Relieved when he freed her hand, Liz said, 'How surprised and delighted Anna will be when she finds you've come back unexpectedly. She hasn't been very well lately, and I've been trying to persuade her to see a doctor. But I think she's the kind of person who is terrified of being ill and would rather ignore her symptoms than be told she has something serious. Perhaps you can persuade her to be sensible.'

With obviously genuine concern, he said, 'I'll go round to her house immediately after breakfast. I'm sorry to hear she's not well. I write to her when I'm away, but although she's a sharp-witted old dear, she's had very little schooling and can't read or write much herself. Even if she could, it would have been difficult for her to keep in touch with me. I've been exploring Australia and the Pacific, with no fixed mailing address.'

About fifteen minutes later, when Liz had scrambled four eggs while he toasted yesterday's bread and made the coffee, they sat down to breakfast at the round wicker table on the upper terrace.

With the broad-brimmed Italian gardener's hat tipped well forward, she sipped the thick juice of the fruit he had liquidised. Peach was the predominant flavour, with traces of cherry and strawberry and the underlying tart tang of lemon. She hoped there would be enough fruit left to make the salad she had planned for lunch. Then she remembered that by lunchtime she would have packed her things and left the villa.

'Why is it called Villa Delphini? I asked Anna, but she didn't know. I assume *delphini* means dolphin, but there seem to be more lions about the place than dolphins.'

'Portus Delphini was the Roman name for Portofino,' he explained. 'The lions are probably a collection made by one of the previous owners of the house, the way some people collect china pugs or cow creamers.'

'How long have you owned the house?'

'About ten years. I came here on a friend's boat, not intending to stay. You see the building on the headland, next to the church?'

'You mean the one with the Latin inscription on the tower?'

'Oh, you've read it, have you?'

'I read it. I couldn't translate it.'

'It's from a verse by the Roman poet Catullus. It means *O what is more blessed than to throw cares aside, as the mind lays down its burden and, weary with labour and far journeys, we come home to our own place.* Whoever had the inscription put up there must have felt Portofino was his place. As, after two weeks, did I.'

'Yet you've been away for two years. Didn't you miss it? Weren't you homesick?'

A curiously sombre expression clouded his deep blue eyes and compressed his wide well-cut mouth with its look of good humour and sensuality.

'At times, yes—very,' he answered. 'But life is short and the world is wide. Anyone who can should see as much of it as possible.' He changed the subject. 'In what way has Anna not been well? What do you think might be the trouble?'

'I'm not sure. It might be gallstones. She's had two very bad bouts of pain, on both occasions following visits from relations who have taken her out for rich meals.'

He had been reserving his fruit juice in order to eat the moist fluffy eggs while they were at their best. The last mouthful swallowed, he touched a napkin to his lips.

'That was delicious,' he told her, with a smiling inclination of his head. 'Are you a nurse by profession, Liz?'

'Heavens, no! I paint for my living.'

In the act of lifting the glass of juice to his lips, he paused, his eyes narrowing suddenly. 'Do you indeed? What sort of things do you paint?'

'I set out to be an illustrator because it didn't seem likely I could make a living painting to please myself. But by incredible luck that's what I've been able to do. Six years ago, when I was twenty-two, I had two pictures accepted for the Summer Exhibition at the Royal Academy in London. They were both bought by an American woman for her Manhattan apartment. They were seen by a New York dealer who commissioned me to paint some more, in the same style. It's gone on from there.'

'You must be exceptionally talented,' was his comment. 'It takes most artists a long time to establish a reputation which will pay the rent. Many of them never achieve that happy condition.'

'I know, and it's not because I'm particularly gifted that I've been able to support myself as a

freelance for the past five years. It's just that the
subjects I choose to paint seem to appeal to a lot of
people with the money to pay quite a lot for a
minuscule painting.'

'Are you a miniaturist?'

'No—or only in the sense that my pictures can be
held in the hand. I don't paint portraits on ivory. I do
very tiny still lifes in oils on canvas. My overheads are
minimal. I use the best possible materials but in very
small quantities and I don't need a studio. I can work
at a kitchen table.'

'I'd like to see some of your work. Have you been
painting while you've been here?'

'Oh, yes, I work every day. That was how I met
Anna. I was sketching down in the *piazza* and she
came and looked over my shoulder and started
chatting. I had a problem understanding her then. I
had some Spanish, but not much Italian. Now, as long
as she speaks slowly, I can understand most of what
she says.'

He pushed back his chair to make room to stretch his
long legs. He was wearing an apple green shirt, white
shorts and a pair of rubber thongs.

'Have you lived in Spain?' he enquired.

'Only for a couple of months. I was there before I
came here. I wanted to visit Florence. While I was
there, some Americans told me about Portofino. It
sounded a good place to spend the summer.'

She realised that he was learning a lot about her but
she still knew little about him. Before she could ask
him if he had an occupation, he said, 'You're a
freelance in every sense, I gather? Not married ... or
otherwise attached?'

'No. I was, but ... not any more.'

'Married?'

'Just "attached". How about you?'

'I seem to have "missed the boat", as they used to say of maiden aunts.'

If he had, it must be by choice, she thought, watching him pour out more coffee. No man as attractive as David Castle would have problems finding a wife. Unless he had given his heart to someone who wasn't available, such as another man's wife.

Evidently it wasn't a subject he wanted to dwell on. He said briskly, 'When she first came to work for me, Anna used to "live in". But she was nervous alone here when I was away, even for short periods. When I decided to take off for an indefinite period, she went back to her house in the village. Maybe you're right about the gallstones, but I wonder if climbing the hill every few days has been too much for her.'

'I don't think there's anything wrong with her heart,' said Liz. 'She's overweight and she has to sit down for a few minutes when she arrives, but then so did I until I got used to coming up by the short cut. Sometimes Anna gets a lift and comes up by the road. She's very conscientious about keeping the house in good order. All the time I've been here she's come every other day. I offered to open the windows so that she only needed to come once a week, but she wouldn't hear of it. I don't think she trusted me to be equally conscientious,' she added, with a grin.

It was the first time she had smiled at him; a smile that transformed her face which, in repose, usually had a reserved, even grave, expression. But when she smiled or laughed the gravity fled and her amber eyes glowed with amusement. Cat's eyes, Richard had called them, and they were not unlike the eyes of a marmalade cat. But whereas cats blinked and looked away when someone tried to hold their gaze, Liz's was direct and steady.

Sometimes she stared at people for too long, making them uncomfortable because they didn't realise she was an artist studying their skin tones or the shape of their features. Several times, in Spain and Italy, she had looked too long at a man who interested her artist's eye and found herself having to brush him off. After two or three such experiences, she had learnt to be careful whom she studied.

'I expect she thought you might be so absorbed in your painting you'd forget such mundane matters as opening and closing windows,' he said, returning her smile. 'She knows that writers and artists tend to lose track of time when they're in the throes of creation.'

'Are you a writer, David?'

'No, but some of my friends are. Most of the people who stay here, or who used to stay here, have creative occupations which they don't necessarily leave behind when they take a holiday. If you'll excuse me, I'll go down and see Anna now.' He swallowed the last of his coffee and rose to his feet.

Pausing on her side of the table, he said, 'I shan't be long. Don't start packing your gear until I come back. If Anna is feeling up to it, I'll get her to come and chaperone you while we find out if sharing the house is a practical proposition. You have a fruit juice moustache.'

Lightly, with the tip of his forefinger, he traced the rim of her upper lip. Then, the soles of his thongs flapping on the time-worn clay tiles with which the terrace was paved, he disappeared into the house.

Presently, having cleared the table and carried the tray back to the kitchen, Liz returned to the terrace in time to catch a glimpse of his fair head at the bottom of the garden. He was going out of sight at a speed which indicated he must have changed the thongs for espadrilles or deck shoes.

Judging that he would be gone for at least an hour, she decided to have the swim she usually had before breakfast. One of the pleasures of life at the villa was being able to swim in the nude when Anna wasn't around to be scandalised by such immodesty. Screened from the road and the grounds of the neighbouring villas by tall cypress hedges, the garden of the Villa Delphini had extensive views of the sea and the rugged coastline, but was itself totally secluded from observation from higher up the hillside.

As she swam up and down the long pool, counting her laps with the aid of a pile of pebbles on the pool deck at the shallow end, she pondered David's suggestion that she should remain at the villa. Proposition was the word he had used. In spite of his mention of chaperonage by Anna, was it, in fact, a proposition in the slang sense? If she stayed, would he take it to mean she was prepared to live with him in both meanings of the term? She wished now she had said no to his question about her status. Now he might have a false impression.

Having swum fifty laps she climbed out, dried herself, and went to the summerhouse where the sailcloth-covered mattresses for the sunbeds were stored. There were half a dozen of the long wooden sunbeds with their wheelbarrow-style handles arranged round the pool deck. Every spring, when David was in residence, they were given a fresh coat of paint by the gardener, Anna had told her. He came twice a week, spending the rest of his time tending the gardens of the other large villas.

Long ago, when Anna was Liz's age, each villa had had several gardeners and a staff of maids. Before the beginning of modern tourism, people had been glad of the work.

At the end of the 1920s, Anna had worked as a

housemaid for some people whose summer house-
parties had included an English lieutenant-colonel
who had recently married a widow with two young
sons. The Italian woman still remembered how much
in love they had been, although long past the first
flush of youth.

'They were so happy together, but their marriage
only lasted ten years. Such a tragedy! She was stung
by a poisonous insect and the doctors couldn't save
her,' Anna had told Liz, during one of her many
reminiscences of Portofino's past. 'He never got over
her death. He didn't marry again. He devoted himself
to the Army and became a very famous man.'

'Do you remember his name, Anna?'

'She called him Bernardo and her name was Betty.
Their surname was Mont . . .gom . . .ery. Many years
later the Queen of England made him a lord, I was
told. He wouldn't be alive today, but perhaps you've
heard of him.'

Liz had heard of Field-Marshal Viscount
Montgomery and the famous Battle of El Alamein in
the Second World War. She had even seen a clip from a
talk he had given on television. But she hadn't known
that behind his abrupt no-nonsense manner lay a
history of love and loss.

It had also come as a surprise to her that Anna, whose
married life had been one of unremitting hardship and
childbearing, should take a vicarious pleasure in the
love affairs and luxurious lives of the people she had
served.

There was no trace of sourness or envy in the
housekeeper's character. She accepted her lot and had
no grudge against those who had been more fortunate.
Perhaps because she was a devout Roman Catholic
and believed implicitly in the rewards of the next life.

Anna's life on earth made Liz glad she had been

born several generations later, in an era when girls didn't have their futures decided for them by their parents or by being rich or poor. Yet although they had almost total freedom now, it still wasn't easy for her and her contemporaries to find lasting love and happiness.

Yesterday the thought of being almost thirty and still on her own had depressed her. Today that glum mood had lifted. She felt full of energy and confidence.

When David returned Liz was doing her yoga *asanas* on an exercise mat in the hall. She had found it impossible to concentrate on work and was exercising now in case it was difficult to do it at her usual time, before supper.

Had she not been expecting him to reappear shortly, his soundless arrival would have startled her. As she had guessed earlier on he was no longer wearing the thongs but a pair of faded red espadrilles. Although he was carrying a large loaded plastic bag and the short cut was a stiff climb, he wasn't out of breath.

'Don't stop on my account,' he said, with an admiring appraisal of her slim, supple figure as she uncoiled from a posture and rose from the mat. She was wearing a short-sleeved white leotard and a pink and white plaited sweatband.

'I've virtually finished. How is Anna today?'

'She seems fine. Later on she's going to come up and cook dinner for us—and also sleep here tonight,' he added. 'She suggested it before I did. It doesn't suit Anna's ideas of propriety that "a nice well brought up young lady like Signorina Redwood" should sleep unprotected with a man in the house. I didn't tell her I arrived in the small hours, She thinks I flew in this morning. On her instructions I shopped for some extra food,' he added, to explain the bag.

'Your Italian is fluent, I imagine,' said Liz, pulling off the sweatband and finger-combing the light fringe which fell almost to her eyebrows.

'Fairly fluent . . . by no means perfect. Can I hand this over to you? I want to go and see what sort of shape my car's in. A mechanic from my garage in Rapallo should have been coming over regularly to keep it in order. Let's hope he has.'

While he went off to the coach-house, which she had never seen inside, Liz took the shopping bag to the kitchen. Was this the thin end of the wedge? The first hint that, if she stayed on, gradually he would try to delegate more and more 'feminine' tasks to her.

Could you sew on this button for me, sweetie? Be a dear girl and make some coffee, would you? I've got a hell of a tight schedule today. Would you mind taking my blue suit to the cleaners? Oh, hell, I forgot to organise a wedding present for Larry and Margot. You're not too tied up today, are you? Do you think you could beetle along to Peter Jones? They've a list of the things they want in the Bride's Book, so it shouldn't take more than five minutes to pick something out.

Echoes from her life with Richard came back to her as she unloaded the bag and distributed its contents about the kitchen. No way was she going to allow a similar situation to creep up on her here.

With Anna around, it wouldn't. The housekeeper would press his shirts, replace missing buttons and attend to all the other jobs which generations of women had accepted as part of their natural function. But if Anna's recent symptoms worsened and she became too ill to continue keeping house for David, would he engage a substitute, or would he expect Liz to take over the domestic reins?

What she *would* find acceptable—assuming she

remained at the villa, which she was still debating with herself—was for them to share the chores equally.

But on her last trip to London to confer with her English agent and to have her teeth checked, she had read in a magazine in her dentist's waiting-room an article which had stated that although among couples, married or unmarried, where both partners worked outside the home, men were believed to tackle more of the housework than formerly, recent research had shown that they still did only a very small share of domestic work.

David was attractive and intelligent. If in the next few days he didn't reveal anything off-putting, she believed she could finish her tenancy as planned and find it even more enjoyable than her time alone at the villa. But she must make it clear from the outset that between certain hours every day she had to concentrate on work.

'The car seems fine,' he said, coming into the kitchen. 'I'm going to make some more coffee while you fetch down some of your paintings. Presumably you keep them upstairs?'

'Yes, I do . . . okay,' she agreed.

Running upstairs to her bedroom—his bedroom now—she opened the cupboard where she kept her working equipment and took out the two small paintings she had had framed in Rapallo last week.

One was of a saucer of olives, a glass of white wine and a crust of bread lying on a blue-checked napkin. The background was a sunlit flagstone, with the glass standing in a patch of shade. The glistening skins of the olives, the condensation on the glass and the velvet texture of the moss growing along the edge of the stone had made it a difficult subject, but she was pleased with the result.

The second painting had been inspired by a needle-case she had found in an antique market in London. It was very old, made of yellowed ivory in the form of a quiverful of arrows with Cupid carved on one side of the quiver and two hearts aflame on the other. It had been expensive, but no more so than the pair of Maud Frizon shoes to which she had also succumbed that day.

She had painted the needle-case with two crested silver livery buttons beside a Victorian glass ink-pot filled with tiny wild flowers on the reflecting surface of a polished wood table.

When she showed the two paintings to David, he showed no immediate reaction, looking carefully at them for some time before he said, 'Would you accept a commission to paint something belonging to me? Or do you only paint your own choice of subject?'

As a respoinse to her work, it was both flattering and disappointing. That he wanted to own a Redwood was gratifying up to a point, but perhaps, after what she had told him, he thought it a good investment.

Liz enjoyed the good living she made, but she also liked to feel that her pictures were valued as more than decorative objects which would appreciate in worth. She hoped that among the Redwoods on both sides of the Atlantic there were at least a few which were among their owners' most cherished personal treasures.

Perhaps it was conceited to think that, and to wish he had shown more feeling about the two she had brought down.

'It would depend what you wanted me to paint,' she answered cautiously. 'Some things—charming in themselves—just don't interest me as subjects. In fact it's becoming harder to find objects which do inspire me.'

He said, 'Later on I'll show you some of my

favourite things. Most of them have been put away during my absence to save Anna unnecessary dusting. By the way, I thought we'd drive down to the *piazza* for lunch and pick her up afterwards. Is that all right with you?'

'You must know half Portofino, if not all Portofino. I don't want to intrude on your reunion with everyone. I'm quite happy to eat up here.'

'I'd rather we ate together. I want to get to know you.'

'You already know a good deal. You're the man of mystery. I don't even know what you do yet. You do something presumably, even if only as a hobby?'

'I do the same thing as you. I paint—not as a hobby. It's been my profession for twenty years.'

She felt sure she had never heard of him, or seen any of his work.

'How strange that Anna didn't tell me,' she said. 'That must be the reason she suggested I should stay here. She has a soft spot for artists.'

'Perhaps. I haven't asked her yet. It was hard to get a word in edgeways. She was much keener to tell me about what's been happening here than to hear about my adventures,' he said, with a smile. 'To her Portofino is the centre of the earth. What goes on in the rest of the world really isn't too important.'

'Don't we all think that at rock bottom? That wherever we are is the hub of the universe? Didn't you feel it on your travels?'

'I felt at the ends of the earth,' he said drily. 'Thousands of miles from the centre of things. I missed seeing houses like this.'

He tilted his chair to look up at the apricot walls and blue-green shutters. On all sides the house was embellished with convincing *trompe l'oeil* stonework surrounds to the windows, as were many of the houses in the region. In some cases sun and rain had weathered away all but traces of the skilful three-dimensional paintwork. Here it was still fairly new and, seen from far down the hill, gave the Villa Delphini the air of a small but noble *palazzo*.

'It isn't until you leave Europe that you realise the *embarras de richesse* of marvellous buildings we have here,' David continued. 'In Australia an historic house usually means something late Victorian. They've pulled down some of their best stuff to make way for roads. As we have in Europe, of course. But we had more in the first place.'

'I worried about that in Spain. Old houses with beautiful *rejas* being bulldozed to make room for ugly blocks of apartments or, if not bulldozed, left to fall into ruin,' said Liz. 'They'll regret it in twenty years' time, when it's too late.'

David rose to his feet. 'This morning I don't want to dwell on the follies of planners and the crimes of developers. I'm going to fetch some champagne to celebrate my homecoming, and the unexpected pleasure of finding a colleague in residence.'

He picked up her right hand and kissed it with the unselfconscious grace with which Latin men performed the gesture. 'You are more than welcome, *bella signorina*.'

An hour later, half a bottle of Perrier-Jouët's Belle Epoque on an almost empty stomach made Liz glad of an opportunity to slip into the kitchen and eat some slices of salami to blot up the champagne.

To go down to the port she changed back into the simple outfit she had put on earlier. She was already wearing the small gold stud ear-rings which she took off only to wash her ears. Now she added the gold chain on which she wore her father's signet ring.

This was the only jewellery she had with her. From the first year of her success she had invested as much as she could spare in antique jewels. But they were in a deposit box in her bank in London. To tote them round Europe with her would have been a worry. Anyway, since leaving Richard she had had no reason to dress up.

David's car, she discovered, was a sleek open-top silver Ferrari, the 308GTSi model which Richard would have liked to own but couldn't afford in addition to the flat in Chelsea, the yacht on the Costa del Sol and a timeshare suite at Stouts Hill, a country house in the Cotswolds.

She knew what the Ferrari cost, and its expensive fuel consumption. It suggested that David Castle must have substantial private means in addition to whatever he made as an artist.

As he put her into the passenger seat and the closing door made the distinctive sound of top-quality coachwork, her interest in him intensified. The champagne hadn't loosened his tongue. He had remained noticeable cagey. Short of asking point blank the things she wanted to know, she had had to contain her curiosity.

'Do you drive, Liz?' he asked, as the sports car glided between the tall stone gateposts, each one topped by a lichened stone lion.

'Yes, I've had a licence for ten years but, living mostly in London, I haven't used it a great deal.'

'Would you drive Anna back later on?'

The thought of being entrusted with the luxurious car when the last vehicle she had driven had been a small Ford Fiesta, rented in Spain to explore the hill towns of Andalusia, was daunting.

'Where will you be?' she asked.

'This only seats two people. I'll walk up.'

'I think it would be better if I walked and you drove Anna. This isn't any old jalopy.'

'Don't let the image scare you. It's a very easy car to drive. The gear change takes a little getting used to and, at night, it has one tricky feature. If you push the dip lever too far, the headlamps retract into the wings. But you won't be using the headlights and there aren't any other pitfalls. All Italian cars handle well, and especially Ferraris.'

Liz decided not to argue the matter now. Later, after wine with their lunch, she could plead—probably with truth—that she had drunk too much to drive.

'Won't you have a problem finding somewhere to park?' she asked. 'By this time of day the car park is usually packed out.'

'I know, and I had a word with the chap in charge of the parking spaces earlier on. He's keeping one for me. I also made sure of a table at my favourite restaurant. But we shouldn't eat too much lunch because Anna will expect us to pack away a mountain of *pasta* this evening. You're not one of those women who refuse to eat *pasta*, I hope.'

'I adore *pasta*—on occasion. I couldn't eat it every day or I'd be the same size as Anna. But as long as I don't feast too often, and keep taking plenty of exercise, I don't have a serious problem.'

'You don't appear to have any problem,' he said, with a swift sideways look at her body and slim sun-tanned legs.

It was a look which reminded her that only a few hours before she had woken up in his arms. Could two people ever have had a more extraordinary introduction?

She had gone to sleep desperately lonely and, like the answer to a prayer, had woken to find herself sharing the great golden bed with one of the most personable men she had ever seen; a man, moreover, who as soon as he was fully awake had handled the situation in the nicest possible way.

Remembering him striding purposefully towards the bathroom, an Apollo with straight sun-streaked hair instead of the stylised curls associated with Greek gods, she knew that already she was strongly attracted to him.

Out of the corner of her eye Liz watched his lean hands steering the car down the tight curves of the rather narrow hill road. He held the wheel firmly but lightly. She was startled to find herself wondering if he made love with the same easy confidence.

There was only one road to Portofino: a narrow, serpentine coast road between the cliffs and the sea. In summer, except very early or very late, it was almost always choked with traffic. However, as Portofino had only a very limited area for parking, and cars were not permitted to intrude on the waterfront, many tourists arrived only to find they must turn back to Santa Margherita and Rapallo.

It was the difficulty of access which had saved the small port from being ruined by modern development. Seen from the sea—Liz had once taken the boat trip to San Fruttuoso, a village accessible only by water or footpath—the tall, narrow houses behind the quays looked like a stage set.

Unlike the white houses of Spain which she had found rather glaring in the strong southern light, the houses of Portofino were painted in restful tones of rose-red, lemon yellow, soft terracotta and peach. Where the quays joined and formed the *piazza* many of the houses had been converted into restaurants with tables, shaded by awnings, spreading over the cobbles.

The table reserved for David had a good view of the quay where the largest yachts and cruisers berthed.

They were shown to it by the proprietor, who greeted him like an old friend and looked with interest at Liz. As did, some minutes later, the proprietor's wife when she bustled out to take their order.

Liz had never minded eating alone. People-watching was one of her favourite pastimes and in Italy a woman on her own was not neglected by the waiters as sometimes happened in other countries. However, after six months of her own company, it was good to be lunching *à deux* with a personable man.

After some discussion, they decided to have only one dish, the *insalata di mare* which David assured her the restaurant did very well. They were sipping white wine and waiting for their seafood to arrive when he suddenly leaned towards her and put out his hand to examine the gold signet ring which hung just short of the vee of her linen top.

As he held the ring between his finger and thumb and turned it to look at the small crest engraved on it, the back of his hand rested against her left breast.

She felt sure it was not a deliberate contact and that he was unaware of it, being intent on studying the ring. But she was intensely conscious of it. It conjured a vivid memory of his tall frame lying behind her, and his warm palm cupping her breast and the nervous thudding of her heart, which began again now, but not because she was afraid.

'A love token, Liz?' he asked, with an uplifted eyebrow.

'In a manner of speaking. It belonged to my father. We were very fond of each other. He died when I was twenty.'

'And your mother?'

'She's alive, but I don't often see her. She lives in Cambridge, Massachusetts, with her second husband. My parents divorced when I was eight. I lived with

Mother for some years and spent holidays with my father. Then, in my teens, Mother found me impossible—as I probably was—and I went to boarding school in England and only spent summer holidays with her and the rest with . . . my father.'

She had hesitated for a second because although James Redwood had always been Daddy to her, and that was how she still thought of him, she felt that at twenty-eight to use that name sounded affected.

Even when she was younger she had taken care to avoid being suspected of being a Sloane Ranger. In America it hadn't mattered; all the young people she knew there were themselves Preppies. But in England none of her fellow art students had come from privileged backgrounds. The fact that by then her father had been living in a gamekeeper's cottage on very little money wouldn't have saved her from being regarded with a certain suspicion and, by some students, with dislike.

'Where did he live?' David asked.

While she was speaking he had let go of the ring and resumed his relaxed position in the red-lacquered basket chair at right angles to hers. With him she could answer frankly without being suspected of being a spoiled, stuck-up snob, which was how a lot of the students regarded girls with her antecedents.

'In Norfolk,' she answered. 'My school had been his grandfather's house and because of that he was able to get me in for reduced fees. The basic reason for my parents' divorce was because Mother thought she was marrying money and status and realised too late that she had miscalculated. All that my father inherited when his father died was a large, draughty house with no up-to-date heating or plumbing and a massive burden of debts. Enough of my life history. Tell me some of yours. Where is your family home?'

'Northamptonshire. I never go there. My widowed sister-in-law lives there with her two daughters. Margaret and I don't get on. The last time I was at Blackmead was over six years ago.'

The withdrawn, brooding expression she had noticed before reappeared. She sensed that the memory of his last visit to Blackmead was in some way a painful one.

Just then a waiter arrived with two plates of seafood. David shook out his napkin and moved his chair closer to the table, whatever had been on his mind dispelled by the appetising lunch being set before them.

Later, after they had helped Anna close up her house and to carry the belongings she wished to bring with her to the car, David insisted Liz should drive up the hill. Although normally a confident driver, in spite of her limited experience, she breathed a sigh of relief on reaching the villa's forecourt with the valuable sports car unharmed.

Richard, had he owned a Ferrari, would never have trusted her to drive it. On his boat he had never suggested she take the helm, although she had learned to crew competently and could have changed places with him, given the opportunity.

Somehow, throughout their time together, she had always played a passive role, agreeing to his plans for weekends and holidays even when she would have preferred to do something different. As she wasn't by nature a passive person she had never understood how it was that she had become one with him. Except that, at the beginning, she had been in love with him and, basking in his love for her, would have done anything to please him.

While Anna was preparing dinner for them, David asked Liz if she would like to see his studio.

Apparently it was the building behind the coach-house which she had assumed was an unused outhouse.

'It's probably thick with dust. I never allow Anna in here,' he said, producing the key.

She had a sinking feeling that although he had claimed to be a professional artist he was actually a dilettante who had managed to sell a few pictures at amateur art shows. Was there anything more difficult than having to make polite remarks about paintings one didn't like?

David unlocked the door and peered inside. 'It's not as bad as I thought.' He gestured for her to precede him.

The building was without windows, but had an enormous skylight, invisible from the garden, with horizontal slatted blinds which, at the touch of a switch, opened and slid to one side, admitting the soft evening light.

Before she had time to look round her eye was caught by a painting on the opposite wall.

'Oh ... you have a David Warren!' she exclaimed delightedly. She had admired Warren's work since she was a student. Then she noticed the two smaller paintings flanking the large one were also Warrens. There were Warrens all round the room. She swung round. 'Are *you* David Warren?'

He acknowledged her startled question with a smiling nod. 'Have you seen my stuff somewhere else?'

'But of course ... you're a famous artist ... far more successful than I am. Why didn't you tell me who you were?'

'You might never have heard of my alter ego. I'm not the kind of painter admired by students and art critics.'

'Do art critics buy many paintings? Certainly

students don't. Curators and connoisseurs are the people who count. They buy you.'

'Fortunately, yes,' he agreed.

He began to wander round the room, pulling out drawers which had not been opened for two years, taking dust covers off easels.

Liz looked more closely at the paintings. The discovery that he was David Warren was oddly unnerving. To be physically attracted to him was one thing; to find that he was one of the ten or twelve living artists whose work she particularly admired was an unforeseen complication.

Presently he took her back to the house and they sat in the frescoed *salone* drinking Chianti until Anna called them to the table.

'Tomorrow I must move my things out of your room,' said Liz, as they finished the meal with figs macerated in *grappa*.

'That isn't necessary. Stay there. All the beds in the house are comfortable. I don't mind where I sleep. Tonight I should sleep like a log if I had to lie on the floor.'

Next morning, while he was still sleeping, she moved out of his room and arranged her possessions in a room on the west side of the villa.

It was almost time for lunch before David appeared, looking much refreshed by his long rest.

In the days that followed his manner towards her was as circumspect when they were alone as it was when Anna was keeping an eye on them. He spent most of his time in the studio or sitting on the terrace dealing with the correspondence which had piled up in his absence. He wrote his replies on a red Olivetti, pecking away at the keyboard with only two fingers, but typing with speed and accuracy.

In the evenings they sat on the terrace, drinking wine or coffee and talking long after Anna had said good night.

Sometimes David talked about his travels, and sometimes they talked about painting, an inexhaustible subject.

Every night they took the glasses and cups to the kitchen and washed them up before David checked the ground floor doors and windows while Liz climbed the staircase ahead of him. And every night when she said, 'Good night, David,' and he replied, 'Good night, Liz,' she had a strong intuition he didn't want to say good night to her.

There was something in the way he looked at her when he added, 'Sleep tight,' that told her he was as strongly attracted to her as she was to him. But for a reason she could only guess at, he was choosing to play a waiting game.

As obviously he wasn't a shy man, she hoped the reason might be that he saw her as something more than a passable female who might be willing to have a pleasant affair with him.

When two weeks had passed since his return to the villa, Liz was forced to admit to herself she was falling in love with him; indeed had already fallen.

This time, she felt, the man who had captured her heart was in every way worthy of love. What troubled her was the fact that he was still a bachelor. Any man still unmarried at his age must have a special reason for his single status. And none of the reasons that she reviewed in her mind augured well for him taking her seriously.

If and when he stopped playing the waiting game and attempted to take their relationship across the safe threshold of friendship into the perilous realm of a sexual relationship, how should she respond?

Of course if he suddenly said, 'Liz, I've fallen head over heels in love with you. Will you marry me?' there would be no problem. She'd answer, at once, 'Need you ask?' and fall joyously into his arms.

But, alas, that was wishful thinking, most unlikely to be realised. Men no longer proposed to women on the basis of a proven rapport and an untested physical attraction.

Contemporary love *à la mode* went through three stages. First, bed. If that was all right, living together. Then, if that was successful for a year or two, finally, eventually, marriage. Or, 'Too bad it didn't work out.'

Undoubtedly it was a system which circumvented a great many ill-judged marriages and subsequent divorces. But it wasn't without its own pitfalls; the main one being that a man didn't have to commit himself. Which was fine for a woman equally wary of commitment, but made for an uneasy situation for someone sure that, at last, she had found the man of her dreams.

How many women, however liberated, took the initiative in saying, 'I love you. Can we stay together for life?'

Not many, Liz suspected. Certainly she could never do it. Unless David made it patently clear that he loved her, she couldn't expose her own feelings.

Which left her confronting the dilemma of how to react if he tried to persuade her to return to the romantic golden bed with its flower-wreathed pillars and the arms of an Italian duke carved on the front of the canopy.

Cooking delicious meals for them, Anna was in her element. Her cuisine was simple peasant fare, but made with the freshest ingredients and seasoned with fresh herbs.

'The secret of Anna's good cooking is the oil she uses,' David told Liz. 'It comes from Lucca. The first pressing of the olives gives a greenish oil with a wonderfully fresh fruity flavour. It's the best olive oil in the world.'

He had been at home for three weeks when their conversation before lunch was interrupted by the distant sound of breaking china.

'It's unlike Anna to drop things. Excuse me a moment.' He rose and headed for the kitchen.

Liz followed. They found Anna lying on the floor in a mess of shattered earthenware and scattered *antipasto*, her sallow face grey with pain.

Later, Liz wondered how she would have coped had David not been there to telephone the nearest doctor and to talk reassuringly to Anna in his fluent Italian. With him in charge of the situation all Liz had to do was to fetch a pillow and blankets and to clear up the mess which, even in her pain, was a source of distress to the sick woman.

Within an hour of the doctor's arrival an ambulance had been summoned and Anna was on her way to a hospital in Genoa for tests. David and Liz followed in the Ferrari.

It was late afternoon when they left her. David would have paid for a private room but, discussing this on the way there, Liz said she felt his housekeeper would be less nervous in a public ward with other patients.

Shortly before they said goodbye to her, Anna said something to David, speaking too rapidly for Liz to catch more than the name Rapallo.

'She says she has a cousin in Rapallo who will keep house for us while she's in here and chaperone you,' he explained. He wrote down the address Anna gave him.

The sun was beginning to sink as they drove back along the *autostrada* through a series of tunnels in the wooded hills. It was only a ten-minute drive from the outskirts of Genoa—Genova on the signboards—to the sliproad leading to Rapallo.

All afternoon Liz had been too concerned about Anna to give any thought to the fact that her illness meant that tonight, for the first time since his unexpected return, Liz and David would be alone in the house between sunset and sunrise.

Not that Anna's presence at the villa would have prevented them from spending the night hours together had they wanted to. Nevertheless there was a subtle difference between having her with them and having the villa to themselves.

As he drove through the back streets of Rapallo in the direction of the palm-lined promenade overlooking the town's crescent beach and, passing the northern end of the sea front, joined the stream of cars heading for Santa Margherita, she wondered if David had forgotten about Anna's cousin.

Or if he had no intention of enlisting her services.

CHAPTER TWO

ALTHOUGH Liz had thought a great deal about the decision she might have to make sooner or later, she still wasn't sure what to do if and when David made a pass at her.

She had always felt one of the best things about living in the last quarter of the twentieth century was that, once a woman had given her heart to a man, she could also give him the pleasure of making love to her without the fear of pregnancy and society's disapproval which had loomed over lovers like dark clouds in previous generations.

Yet even without those restraints, the cause of so much feminine anguish in the past, there were still things to be considered before taking the plunge.

Was it too soon to be *sure* she loved David? How did he feel about her?

Was he looking for love and marriage, or only a casual affair? If she made a free gift of herself would he value her less than if she held out, not for marriage, as women had once, but at least for a declaration of love from him?

Richard had *told* her he loved her, but he hadn't really; not if loving meant putting as much value on another person's needs as on one's own. Not only had he not taken her work seriously, but he hadn't even made sure that when they made love it was always as good for her as it was for him.

That was something else that troubled her. Supposing she let David make love to her only to find him as selfish and unimaginative as Richard? It was easy, loving him, to persuade herself he would be a marvellous lover. But, more from what she had read and been told by other women than from her own very limited experience, she had come to the conclusion that good lovers were rare.

Could she take the disappointment of finding out the man beside her was not especially skilled or sensitive?

Did the fact that he painted pictures showing understanding and tenderness necessarily mean that he demonstrated those qualities in his relations with women?

One of his finest paintings, of which she possessed a colour copy taken from a book on contemporary aritsts, was a picture of two old women dressed entirely in black from the scarves which covered their white hair to the cheap slippers on their swollen feet. They were sitting on a bench outside a whitewashed cottage, gossiping. It could have been painted in any of several Mediterranean countries. They were typical of a generation soon to die out; women whose hard, simple lives had been part of a pattern almost unchanged for centuries.

Thinking about that picture and also of how kindly he had dealt with Anna, promising to visit her every day, calmed some of Liz's doubts about entrusting herself to him—if he wanted her.

Even so, as the car snaked round the bends at the foot of the steep escarpments and each bend brought them nearer to Portofino, she was still uneasy and apprehensive.

When they came to the fork where one way led to the Villa Delphini and the other to the port, he surprised her by not taking the hill road.

'I don't know about you but, not having eaten since breakfast, I'm famished. Let's have a meal at Luigi's place, shall we?'

Until he suggested eating, she hadn't realised she was hungry. At the thought of some food and wine her spirits rose. No wonder she'd had the jitters! After the trauma of Anna's collapse in the kitchen, followed by the trip to hospital with its lowering reminders of her father's premature death, it wasn't surprising she'd had an attack of cold feet.

'That's a great idea,' she agreed, relieved to have their return to the villa postponed for an hour or two.

There were no vacant spaces in the car park. David switched off the motor and unclipped his seatbelt. 'I'll leave the keys with Marco.'

But instead of opening his door he leaned towards her. Before she knew what was happening, his hand was at the back of her neck and his lips were on hers in a long, soft, sensuous kiss.

By the time he took his mouth away the parking attendant was standing by the Ferrari, watching with unabashed interest what was happening inside it.

David swung himself out of the driving seat and exchanged the usual pleasantries with him on his way round to open the door for Liz, who was still in a daze.

As they strolled down to the *piazza* he held her hand firmly in his; and from time to time he looked down at her, a smile lurking in his blue eyes and at the corners of the mouth which had worked such strong magic on her.

It took them two hours to have supper. They started with *cannellini*, the white kidney-shaped Tuscan beans, eaten cold, dressed with oil and vineagar and mixed with thinly sliced onions and chopped parsley. Liz had never tasted anything more delicious than this simple starter, accompanied by good red wine and crusty bread with which to mop round the dish.

For the main course they chose *fusili*, pasta cooked with leeks, ham, cream and Parmesan.

After which she put a hand on her middle and said, with a sigh of satisfaction, 'I shall have to fast for two days now, but who cares? That was a banquet.'

He signalled the waiter and asked for another bottle and something else.

'You haven't ordered a pudding after what we've eaten already?'

'There's something else you must try. Not a pudding, a savoury.'

'David, I can't—not possibly. You must have hollow legs!'

But when the waiter returned with Gorgonzola on toast, after her first bite of the hot, blue-veined ewe's milk cheese, she had to agree it made a splendid conclusion to the meal.

Later they wandered along the quay, past the large and small pleasure craft. There was one very large costly yacht on which the owner was giving an al fresco dinner party attended by several stewards in starched white uniform jackets.

The men sitting round the table were much older than David. The girls were Liz's age and younger, all glamorously dressed and with the sleek pampered look of women whose time is largely devoted to their appearance. Listening to the men's loud guffaws at some witticism, she felt a mental shudder at the thought of the services the girls had to provide in return for their luxurious lifestyle.

Once, at Puerto Bañus in Spain, she had sat in a waterfront café listening to two girls discussing the sexual proclivities of the two elderly men who had subsequently joined them for lunch and who had undoubtedly paid for the parcels the girls had amassed while shopping in nearby Marbella.

Richard, when she had reported some of their conversation to him, had roared with laughter.

'They're seeing the world and enjoying life. What's so terrible about that? If I were a girl, with the looks to attract a rich protector, I'd prefer swanning round the Med to a boring, badly paid job or pushing a pram in the suburbs,' had been his comment. 'It's easy for you to look down your nose at them. You can afford to shop in Marbella with your own money. Those poor little bitches can't.'

'I don't look down my nose at them,' she had protested. 'I just know that, no matter what, I couldn't live off an old man I didn't love, or even a young one for that matter.'

'As long as you keep turning out saleable pictures, you won't have to. Now, having picked up some tips from a couple of professionals, why not try them out on me?'

That conversation, pushed to the back of her mind until now, had been one of the many hair-line cracks in their disintegrating relationship. The final break-up had come after a Marbella party which she had insisted on leaving when people began to snort coke.

Richard had been livid with her. 'Nobody would have forced you to try it,' he had stormed. 'We could have left later on, without a big song and dance. I don't particularly like any of that set, but some of them could be useful to me. I see no point in offending them.'

'I didn't make the fuss, Richard. That was your fault for not leaving when I wanted without a big argument. You know how I feel about drugs. You ought to have known I'd walk out . . . and walked out with me. But the fact is you'd turn a blind eye to any corruption if the people involved might be useful. If you want to know the truth, I can't stand those people—never could. I don't like Marbella. I don't like Puerto Bañus. What I long to see is the real Spain, not just this hideous excrescence along the Costa del Sol.'

'If it's as hideous as that, I wonder so many top people choose to have villas here,' had been his sarcastic retort.

'What top people? Ageing queers? Fading film stars? A few European aristocrats clinging to meaningless titles? There are no really top people down here. Top people like peace and quiet. They couldn't care less about having their photographs in the *Marbella Times*. All one ever meets here are drones and people like you, social climbers.'

Of course she had been exaggerating. There were still some civilised people living in the area, although fewer than twenty years earlier when there had been no rash of new villas on the low green hills of the hinterland.

Having lost her temper and pointed out all that she found displeasing about him, there had been nothing to do but pack her case and take a taxi to El Fuerte, the dignified hotel patronised mainly by Spaniards, in the centre of Marbella.

Next morning she had rented a car and driven away from the resorts into the wild high country of the Sierrra de Ronda, there to mourn the end of a partnership she had once thought would be for life.

It was vexing that the happy mood in which she had left the restaurant had been displaced by all these unpleasant memories conjured by the sight of those girls on the opulent yacht from Marseille. Unaware how plainly her thoughts were reflected in her expression, unless she was trying to hide them, Liz was surprised when David put an arm round her shoulders.

'What's worrying you?'

She mustered a smile. 'Nothing, David.' Seeing he would not be satisfied with that disclaimer, she added, 'Something suddenly reminded me of a bad time in my life ... one I don't want to remember now that I'm having a good time.'

She slipped her arm round his waist and, loosely embraced, they returned towards the *piazza*, there to make for the narrow street which led to the back of the town and the square where cars parked.

At the villa he unlocked the main door and switched on some interior lights before returning to the courtyard to garage the Ferrari.

'Let's have some more coffee, shall we?' he suggested, before he went outside.

In the kitchen Liz filled the percolator and put it on the electric hob which had usurped the function of the huge wood-burning range used in earlier times.

A few minutes later she heard him re-enter the house and lock and bolt the outer door. But he didn't come to the kitchen until the coffee was ready and by that time, from the *salone*, came the slow throb of Hawaiian guitars.

'Let me carry that.' David took the tray from her. As they crossed the hall, he said, 'I'm not much help to the tourist souvenir trade. All I brought back from my travels were half a dozen cassettes picked up en route. Unfortunately the days when a traveller could bring back a genuine Fijian war club, or something equally interesting, are more or less over. In Sydney I was taken to a gallery specialising in aboriginal paintings, but I can't say they appealed to me much.'

'I thought in Australia the thing to buy was opals?'

'So I believe; but not, at that time, having a woman in my life I didn't bother. If I'd know you were waiting for me ...' He smiled at her over his shoulder before he put down the tray.

The guitars were joined by a man's voice singing a Hawaiian love song.

'This is a guy called Don Ho. It's good music to play at a party until the conversation gets going, or to dance to when the party is winding down.' David crossed the room to take glasses and a bottle of brandy from a painted green and gold cupboard.

The singer's accent was American, but some of the words were in the language of the islands. Liz settled herself at the end of a large cushion-heaped sofa, one slim brown foot swinging in time to the lazy rhythm of the song.

'Did you get to Tahiti?' she asked. 'That's the island I long to see.'

'Yes, I spent several weeks there.'

As he poured out the coffee and filled the liqueur glasses, he talked of the lovely French islands where it was always summer.

Liz listened, amazed at her calmness when she knew she was poised on the brink of something momentous. Ever since David had kissed her, her earlier doubts had been replaced by a tranquil sense of inevitability. She was not a fatalist. She had never believed that everyone's life was predestined and there was little one could do to alter the basic pattern. She felt sure there was no pattern; that life went this way or that because of a series of chances.

Yet tonight she could almost believe that the chance encounter with the Americans who had told her about Portofino had been arranged by the Fates, the three goddesses who, in past ages, had been thought to decide the course of each human life.

The music was still playing softly. David rose from his end of the sofa. 'Let's dance.'

She went into his arms.

At first he held her quite loosely, looking down into

her eyes with that hint of a smile in his own. Then, slowly, he drew her closer, putting the hand he was holding on to his shoulder, leaving himself with both hands free to press her against him.

His cheek warm against her temple, their bodies sealed together, Liz closed her eyes and gave herself up to the pleasure of being held in strong arms after the long months alone.

As the sexy voice of Don Ho crooned a refrain, she gave a luxurious sigh and slipped her hands over David's shoulders and across the broad muscular back till her arms were right round his neck.

His hands wandered over her back and she felt his mouth brush her temple and slide downwards over her cheekbone, past her ear, to the side of her neck.

'You smell wonderful,' he murmured, inhaling the lingering fragrance of the *Shalimar* she had put on before lunch.

Pleased she had splurged on the long-lasting scent rather than the evanescent toilet water, Liz drew in her breath as he started to kiss the sensitive skin of her neck.

Her hair was still in its plait instead of in loose silky skeins or a sophisticated coil as it usually was in the evening, at least since his homecoming. He gripped the thick strawberry blonde rope and gently pulled her head backwards, exposing the front of her throat to the hungry heat of his mouth.

She shivered, arching her neck to allow him to reach the tender flesh under her chin.

Behind her, his hands were undoing the buttons which fastened her sun-dress. His fingers caressed her bare spine and came to the clip of her bra.

'Do you need all these clothes on?' he muttered.

She gave a soft gurgle of laughter. 'I think we're both overdressed!' With hands which lacked the sure touch she brought to her work, she fumbled to undo his shirt.

They had been barely moving before. Now they stopped all pretence of dancing. The music played on, ignored. The poured coffee cooled, forgotten. Liz was aware of nothing but the hurried beating of her heart, her increasingly rapid breathing and the hot, pulsing excitement in the core of her body.

As well as buttons at the back, her dress had buttons on the shoulders. He undid them and pushed her away. The cool sleeveless cotton shift slithered softly to the floor. Moments later her bra had followed it and his hands had taken the place of the flimsy lace cups.

His first gentle unhurried caresses made her gasp with pleasure. She felt something happening inside her like the ripening of melons left on a sunny window ledge. Only this was happening all at once. As his fingers explored her smooth flesh, her breasts seemed to swell, her body to fill with sweet juice.

David bent down, his lips closing softly over the tip of her breast. She gave a convulsive shudder, her hands clenching on his shoulders, gripping tight handfuls of shirt as the sensuous movements of his mouth sent electrifying shafts of sensation shooting along every nerve.

The next morning she overslept. When she went downstairs David was cooking his breakfast.

He put his arm round and kissed her. 'I've telephoned the hospital. Anna had a good night. They'll be doing various tests this morning, but we can see her this afternoon.'

'There are some things she'll need. Could we do some shopping in Rapallo and maybe have lunch there?' she asked.

'Why not?'

The day before, in a hurried search of the housekeeper's room for things she would need in hospital, Liz had found little to pack but two voluminous nightgowns, slippers, a missal and Anna's rosary.

In Rapallo she went to a shop which specialised in exquisite lingerie.

'You'll have to come in with me. I need an interpreter,' she told David.

He showed no reluctance to enter a place devoted to women's things. But when, with his help, she explained what she wanted and the proprietress produced a large but fine quality nightdress and matching bedjacket, he said, 'Liz, do you realise the price of things here? Anna buys her clothes in the market. Will she appreciate this quality?'

'Of course she will, David. She's a woman. The fact that she's always had to make do with cheap rubbish doesn't mean she's never yearned for nicer things. All her life she's been washing and ironing lovely clothes for other women. It's time *she* had something lovely. Don't worry: I can afford it. I'm not expecting you to pay for these.'

'That was not my concern,' he said shortly. 'I just don't want you to waste your money. If Anna were thirty years younger——'

His reply took her back in time to the several occasions when Richard had poured cold water on what he considered ill-judged extravagance on her part.

Once, finding her writing a cheque in response to a famine appeal, he had said, 'My dear girl, you do realise, I suppose, that only about a penny of that will actually benefit the starving masses. The rest will either be siphoned off in adminstrative costs at this end or help to buy a Mercedes for some corrupt official at the receiving end.'

Perhaps his cynicism had been well founded, but later she had regretted being persuaded to tear up the cheque. Richard had often stopped her from doing what she wanted to do. But he himself had never refrained from an action because she didn't agree with it.

However much she loved him, she knew it would be very foolish ever to let David develop the same power over her. In future she mustn't forget that in the best close relationships the people involved didn't chip away parts of each other's personalities.

With this in mind, she said lightly but firmly, 'Age has nothing to do with it. An old lady I knew in England once told me that inside herself she didn't feel seventy-three. She still felt a young woman. Sometimes she couldn't believe the face in the mirror was hers. I suspect a lot of older women feel that way.'

Her next call was to a *farmacia* where she bought toilet water and talcum powder, dry and wet tissues, a light hand mirror, a hairbrush and a large blunt-toothed comb to replace Anna's small scratchy comb which might hurt the housekeeper's scalp if it became necessary for someone else to do her hair for her.

When David suggested that next they should go to a florist for some flowers, Liz said, 'Actually a flowering pot plant might be better. It would last longer than cut flowers and save the staff having to find a vase and arrange them, which they don't always have a flair for.'

'I'm sure you're right. I hadn't thought of that aspect,' he said. 'I haven't had much experience of hospital visiting. Evidently you have.'

'My father was in and out of hospitals for several years before he died. At the end he went into a hospice where they were very good to him. I wasn't freelancing then. I had a nine-to-five job so I couldn't nurse him myself. I've always regretted not taking six months off, but I felt if I gave up my job I might not get another. Jobs were hard to come by at that time. How long did it take you to establish yourself, David?'

'I was thirty before I made much impact. I had a small income left to me by my mother which kept the wolf from the door—just! I ate a lot of baked beans and tuna sandwiches for a time. Then I got fed up with that and taught myself to cook a decent meal. I cook pretty well now. How about you?'

'I've been cooking for myself since I've been here, but I like a lot of salads. I rarely eat meat. I don't think most men would be thrilled with my choice of menus,' she added, remembering Richard's dislike of what he called 'rabbit food'.

David said, 'At the moment I've too much work on hand to take over the cooking, and you're busy too, so I think I'll get Anna's cousin to come over three times a week and feed us and clean the place. The rest of the time we can eat out. Does that plan suit you?'

'It sounds fine—as long as you let me make an appropriate contribution to whatever you pay her,' she added. Because he looked as if he might argue the point, she forestalled him. 'Look at the situation in reverse. Would you be happy for me to pay for your keep?'

'I shouldn't object to being your guest as well as your lover,' he said, smiling. 'I'd buy you a case of champagne from time to time, or a side of smoked salmon. The usual guestly gesture.'

At this point they arrived at the flower shop and the conversation had to end. They didn't resume it on leaving because the way back to the car was along a crowded street where he frequently had to fall back and allow her to precede him. By the time they reached the car he had obviously forgotten the subject, because he put on a tape of Luciano Pavarotti, the

Italian tenor, singing a duet with America's Leontyne Price.

They were two of the world's most beautiful voices and Liz had no difficulty in recognising them. She loved music and never travelled without a small portable player and several favourite cassettes to which, like David on his travels, she usually made some additions.

However, as the Ferrari sped along the *autostrada* and Pavarotti's glorious tenor was followed by that of Placido Domingo, her thoughts reverted to David's last remark before they entered the flower shop.

His reference to 'the usual guestly gesture' seemed to suggest that he didn't see their relationship going on for very long; no longer than the visit of a house guest which was seldom more than a few weeks. Yet when she had woken that morning, happy and hopeful after their first night together, 'for ever' had had a new meaning.

They found Anna in better spirits than Liz had expected, considering her previous attitude to hospitals. Luckily there was a woman of similar age and background in the bed alongside the housekeeper's and she had succeeded in dispelling many of Anna's fears.

She was delighted with the pale pink azalea when David put it on the night stand and removed the protective paper. She was pleased with and grateful for the toilet necessities and voluble in her thanks.

But when she opened the box containg the nightgown and jacket, words failed her. With hands calloused and coarsened by a lifetime of housework, she lifted the pin-tucked and lace-trimmed nightdress from its nest of tissue and gazed at it in silence.

Then, to Liz's dismay, her mouth started to quiver and her brown eyes filled with tears.

David's reaction to this might not have met with the approval of the rather severe-looking nurse in charge of the ward. But it made Liz like him all the more.

He perched on the bed at Anna's side, put a comforting arm round her shoulders and gave her his handkerchief in which to bury her face for a few moments before she was ready to mop her eyes and break into a flood of Italian.

'What was all that about?' Liz asked, when Anna paused for breath.

'She was saying that if I had any doubts about why she invited you to stay at the villa, it should be clear to me now. You are not only beautiful to look at, but you have a nature to match. She had watched you and heard about you from people in the port. It was her opinion, with which everyone in Portofino agreed, that you were of a disposition not often found in young girls nowadays,' David interpreted.

'Oh, goodness, what an encomium!' exclaimed Liz, trying to laugh off her embarrassment.

Anna said something else, signing that she wished him to translate it. When she and Liz were alone, she remembered to speak slowly. With David she didn't.

'She says, if you wouldn't think it a familiarity, she would like to give you a kiss,' he explained.

Liz was seated on a chair on the opposite side of the bed. At once she jumped up and offered Anna her cheek, at the same time giving her a hug and kissing her seamed cheek.

As she sat down again, Anna gave a David a nudge and said something to which he responded with noticeable reserve.

Liz had always been quick to catch nuances. Although she hadn't understood the words they had spoken, it was clear to her that Anna had been doing some none too subtle matchmaking, hence David's guarded reaction.

Foreseeing that at any moment Anna would enquire about her cousin, Liz mustered her Italian to enquire what tests the housekeeper had had so far and what the hospital food was like.

This successfully deflected Anna from asking about her cousin, and her account of all that had happened to her in the past twenty-four hours continued until a nurse came to take her to another part of the hospital for further tests.

Later that day David arranged two sunbed mattresses side by side in a corner of the lower terrace and they made love in the sun.

It was one of the days when the gardener didn't come, and no one else was likely to disturb their seclusion. Even so when they first lay down on the mattresses Liz felt rather inhibited by the unlikely chance of an intruder appearing.

But it didn't take David long to make her forget everything but the bliss of abandoning herself to the sun and to him.

At that hour of the day it was too hot to stay locked in each other's arms after their passion was spent. David rolled away from her and, hands clasped, they both dozed for a while.

She woke up to find he had been up to the house to fetch a bottle of champagne and a basket of nectarines.

'I should be working. We should both be working,' she murmured as, still naked, they sat at the edge of the pool, dangling their legs in the water, sipping the chilled champagne and eating the sweet juicy flesh of the nectarines.

'On Monday, at nine o'clock sharp, we'll do that. For the rest of this week let's concentrate on life's other pleasures. With luck we shall still be able to paint in old age, but we may not be able to spend afternoons doing this . . . or that.' He gave a nod in the direction of the mattresses.

'They say people can make love all their lives, if they keep it up,' Liz said idly, watching the gleaming golden reflections in the pool.

'Probably they can. I hope so. But I think by the time you're seventy you may prefer soft lights to sunlight,' he added drily. 'Is there some sun cream in your basket?'

She was using a small straw basket instead of a bag to contain the few things she needed to carry around with her.

'Yes, there is. I put some on earlier.'

'It might be wise to use some more. I'll get it for you.'

She was pleased that he brought the basket from where she had left it and didn't attempt to search for the cream himself. There was nothing private in the basket, but she wouldn't have liked it if he had rooted around as she had once found Richard looking in her bag for a nail file he wanted to use to turn a small screw. She had been even more annoyed when he had criticised her for keeping a lot of unnecessary junk in it. That had been the cause of their first row.

Beneath the brim of the hat which David had perched on her head when they moved to the pool's edge, a slight frown appeared. She wished unhappy recollections of her past wouldn't keep intruding on her present contentment, reminding her how easily an affair of the heart could turn sour.

The next day David came to an arrangement with Anna's cousin. When, later, they went to the hospital, he could say with truth that she would be looking after them until Anna was well enough to return.

On the third day after her admission, they found her in great agitation, having been told by the doctor in charge of her case that she was indeed suffering from gallstones, as Liz suspected, and would need to have an operation, the sooner the better.

Between them, they had managed to soothe her. Later, David had talked to her doctor who had told him that, in view of the unlikelihood of a woman of Anna's age and type being able to stick to the extremely restricted diet which was the conservative treatment for her condition, an operation was the only recourse. She had a good constitution. There was nothing wrong with her heart or lungs. With all surgery there was some risk, but he foresaw no complications in her case.

That night, in the great gilded bed, Liz watched in the mirror above her a scene such as she had visualised during her nights alone.

Lying with her head on David's shoulder, she no longer envied the uncounted, unknown lovers who had shared the vast bed in the past. Now it was her turn to be happy and, judging by the smile on his face as their eyes met in the mirror, he shared her feelings.

Hours later, during the night, she woke up to find herself alone. Thinking David must have gone to the bathroom, she lay listening to the quietness and waiting for him to come back.

When he hadn't returned after quite a long time, she wondered if he could be ill. He had eaten mussels for supper. She had chosen *calamari*. Mussels worried her. While in Spain, she had been told that along parts of the coast hepatitis was endemic, spread by polluted mussels. Since then she'd avoided eating them and had mentioned her reasons to David. He had said that as far as he knew they were safe to eat in Portofino.

But apart from the risk of a liver infection, shellfish could cause bad stomach upsets. Concerned that he might have been stricken by one of these, she jumped out of bed and hurried across to the bathroom.

She found it in darkness. When she switched on the light, the door to the lavatory at the far end was ajar. There was no one there. Perhaps he was using one of the other lavatories.

Wrapping a dry bath towel round herself, she went to look for him.

As soon as she opened the bedroom door, she saw by a shaft of light at the far end of the landing that he must be in one of the bedrooms she had never entered.

Her bare feet making no sound on the polished marble floor, she approached the lighted room. The door was far enough open for her to see, as she neared it, that David was sitting in a chair. He was wearing a navy silk dressing gown with a dark red piping round the collar and cuffs. His feet were thrust into dark red leather mules. He showed no sign of being ill.

There was a glass of water in his hand, but although she stood peering at him for at least a full minute, he didn't raise it to his lips. He seemed to be lost in thought; and whatever was on his mind was making him look a different person from the carefree man who had made love to her a few hours ago.

At intervals, during the time since they became lovers, she had had the feeling that her life had suddenly taken on a dream-like quality. To meet a man she had long admired as an artist and to find him good-looking, nice, funny and terrific in bed was like a fairy-tale. It was too good to be true. In real life nothing was perfect. There had to be something wrong somewhere; a flaw yet to be uncovered.

As she lurked on the shadowy landing, watching

David staring at nothing, she knew her instinct had been right.

A man without any problems did not get up in the night and sit by himself with that troubled expression on his face.

CHAPTER THREE

She moved forward, into the room. 'Can't you sleep?'

David must have very steady nerves. Her question didn't make him jump as she would have in his place.

As he turned his head towards her, the look of sorrow or regret disappeared from his face. He smiled. 'I'm afraid I've always been a bit of an insomniac. I often get up in the night and potter about for an hour. Sometimes I work or read until I feel sleepy again. What woke you up?'

'I don't know. Perhaps not having you curled round behind me. When I found you weren't there, I thought you might be suffering some ill effects from the mussels.'

'No, my stomach feels fine.' He raised the glass and drank some water.

Liz glanced round the room. Behind the bed hung a large piece of antique tapestry depicting a classical scene which she didn't recognise. The furniture included a writing table. As in all the bedrooms there were tall glazed double doors giving on to a balcony.

She wondered why he had chosen this room to sit in. Perhaps for no special reason.

She noticed that lying on the bed was a large roll of stiff paper. It looked like the type of poster she had used to cover as much of the wallpaper as possible in her first bed-sitter in London.

'What's that? May I look?' she asked.

'Go ahead. You may recognise him.'

Liz unrolled the paper. It was a portrait of a man with a smile as secretive and memorable as that of the

Mona Lisa. She had seen the enigmatic black eyes during her visit to Florence.

'It's Lorenzo de' Medici, isn't it?'

David nodded. 'It's from the portrait of him in the Pitti Palace in Firenze.' David used the Italian name for the city. 'Some years ago I had a teenage relation of mine living here for a time. She bought the poster. Lorenzo was Bethany's pin-up.'

'Bethany—what a pretty name!'

'She was a pretty girl.'

'Was?'

'Still is, I imagine. I haven't seen her recently. She's married now . . . busy having babies. You shouldn't be running around barefoot. Come back to bed, *carissima*.'

He swept her up in his arms and carried her to the door, pausing there while she switched off the light.

Liz felt she had to find out what lay behind the look that had been on David's face when he thought himself unobserved.

As they passed the head of the staircase, she said, 'As we're both wide awake, why don't we have some tea? You go down and put on the kettle and I'll fetch my robe and join you in a couple of minutes.'

'I have a better idea. Go back and keep the bed warm and I'll bring some tea upstairs.' He lowered her feet to the floor.

She had brushed her hair and put on her gauzy nightgown when he rejoined her.

Presently, between sips of the subtly-flavoured China tea which they both preferred to Indian tea, she asked him, trying to sound casual, 'David, have you ever been married?' Before he could answer, she added, 'Not many men as nice as you escape the net. But I don't want to pry into your past if you prefer not to discuss it.'

'I've never been married,' he told her. 'Why not? The answer to that, I suppose, is that when I was a young man I fell in love with another man's wife. It was calf love and I got over it, but it took some time. By the time I recovered most of the girls I might have wanted to marry had been snapped up. I was never very eligible from a parental point of view. In the milieu in which I grew up, a younger son wasn't much of a catch, especially a younger son who wanted to paint. Well, you know the form. You grew up in that world as well.'

'Not really. My forebears were country gents, not aristocrats. And we never had any money after my grandfather died. It all went in horrendous death duties. But you became eligible later ... when you inherited the title. Why don't you use it?'

'I already had this house when my brother was killed in an accident. To change my style here would have been a nonsense. Anyway, a title is really more of a liability than an asset nowadays. It puts a lot of people off. They assume you must be a snob. Other people suck up; and sometimes one gets overcharged on the grounds that one must have money. Which, as you know, is often far from the truth.'

'Do you never miss England?' she asked.

'Not a bit. Robert Browning may have preferred buttercups to melon-flowers, but my recollection of April in England is that, if it isn't raining, there's often a piercing east wind lashing those orchard boughs he wrote about so nostalgically. I like it better here.'

She nodded. 'I know what you mean. New England, where my mother's family live, is rather the same—heaven when the weather's good, but terribly dismal when it's pelting with rain. Have you been to America, David?'

'Yes, many times. I like it. New York's a fantastic city. Where is, or was, your base, Liz?'

'London.'

Foolishly, she had allowed Richard to persuade her to move in with him and give up her own flat. It had been a mistake she had resolved never to repeat.

'Before you arrived I was thinking of looking round Greece,' she added. 'Have you been to any of the Greek islands?'

'I travelled all over Europe during my nomadic period. I wouldn't recommend the Greek islands as places to put down roots. They're fine for a holiday . . . a summer. But the plumbing is terrible and houses designed for hot weather can be colder than vaults in winter.' He reached across the table for her hand. 'I'm hoping you're going to stay here for the rest of this summer.'

Only for the rest of the summer? Her heart sank.

Hiding the anxious uncertainty evoked by his remark, she said lightly, 'Yes . . . I'd like that.'

On Sunday, with Liz to help him, David got around to the task of opening cupboards and chests, unearthing all the things put away two years earlier.

At one time he had been an inveterate collector of objects which took his fancy.

'You may not be much of a souvenir-buyer, but you must have spent weeks of your life rummaging around in antique and junk shops to have found this gorgeous miscellany,' she said, watching him open yet another chest of treasures.

'Mm, I suppose I have. Junk-hunting is my second favourite pastime.'

'What's the first?'

He turned and took her face between his hands. 'Silly question!' He kissed her.

It was one of those kisses which began as a light, tender gesture and suddenly caught fire.

Liz struggled free from what threatened to be a long interruption to the task of returning his things to their places. It wasn't that she didn't want to take time out to make love. But she felt that if they did it too often he might become sated, bored with her.

For that reason she pulled away, saying laughingly, 'David, we mustn't slack off. Tomorrow's a working day, remember? What's in that box?' She pointed to the large cardbox box which lay uppermost inside the chest.

To her disappointment, he allowed himself to be deflected. 'It's a piece of fan coral; very brittle and fragile. It belongs in your bathroom. Somebody, years ago, brought it back from Madagascar. I bought it in a shop near Blackmead. It was the label "from Madagascar" that attracted me. It was one of those magic places like Valparaiso, Istanbul and Genoa which I wanted to see when I grew up. Genoa is the only one of them I've been to. Not the romantic city I had imagined. Maybe it's just as well to keep my illusions about the others.'

At the end of a happy day in which she had seen many things she wanted to paint, Liz lay in the huge marble bath, up to her neck in warm water.

David had called it her bathroom because he was using another.

'I know most women prefer separate bathrooms if they're available,' he had said to her.

Wondering from whom he had learned this, she had agreed that it was one of life's nicest luxuries not to have to share washing facilities. In spite of repeated requests, Richard had never bothered to clean the bath at his flat, or anywhere else they had stayed together.

Sometimes, after clipping his toenails, he had left bits of nail on the floor. To Liz, fastidiously neat in her personal habits, sharing a bathroom with him had been a considerable trial.

However, with David who, contrary to the popular myth that most artists were disorganised and slovenly, was a man who tidied up after himself, she felt it would have been pleasant to see his tall frame through the glass walls of the shower cabinet while she lay relaxing in scented water.

As she was wondering if he would ever reveal the whole truth about himself, she remembered how, on his first morning at home, he had admitted to mistaking her for someone else.

She had never pressed him about the identity of that other woman. Perhaps if she did he might feel moved to confide the cause of that sorrowful look she had seen on his face the other night.

Insomnia was, she felt sure, almost always a sign of some deep-seated mental disturbance; some weight on the subconscious mind. A man without cares slept the night through, particularly after making love.

It wasn't until the evening of the day of Anna's operation that Liz mustered the nerve to ask David about the other woman.

Not having been to the hospital that afternoon, they had not seen each other since breakfast. David had spent the whole day closeted in his studio where he was sorting and filing all the sketches made on his trip. He had a system which enabled him to retrieve, in a matter of moments, sketches made years before.

'I can't stand muddle,' he had told Liz.

The efficient arrangement of his studio was essential to an artist whose finished paintings were the outcome of twenty or thirty preliminary sketches.

While he had been busy in the studio, Liz had been equally busy in a shady corner of the garden. In addition to her usual pictures, she was writing and illustrating the adventures of a ship's cat.

At one o'clock Teresa had brought her a bowl of soup and some fruit and had taken the same lunch to David. But although Liz had had several swims during the day, he had remained in seclusion. Not until almost six had he emerged from his work-place to swim twenty strenuous laps before joining her for a happy hour.

Now, as they lingered on the terrace, after a light evening meal prepared by Teresa, she ventured the question which had been on her mind for some time.

'David . . . who did you think was in bed with you that first morning?'

Prepared for a displeased reaction, even a crushing snub, she was relieved when he said at once, 'Francine Valery . . . someone who lived here some years ago.'

The quick candour of his reply made it clear that he had no hang-ups relating to the French girl.

Liz felt encouraged to ask, 'Lived *with* you, d'you mean?'

David nodded. 'She was a fantastic cook and a very nice person. She was here at the same time as Bethany. But she had a restless nature—Francine, I mean—and one day she upped and left. I've never seen her since.'

'Were you in love with her?'

'No. I was very fond of her. She was four years older than I and still married to a Frenchman. They'd had no children and after some years of marriage she had found him boring and left him to go to America where she had a married sister. I met her when she came to Portofino as cook on a yacht. The skipper had begun to make a nuisance of himself. She jumped at the chance to come and cook for me for a while. She was useful with Bethany as well. My niece had come from a home where she was an unwanted stepchild. She needed to come under the influence of someone like Francine ... someone kind and understanding.'

'You are both those,' said Liz, smiling at him.

'I hope so ... but I'm a man. A teenage girl needs someone of her own sex to confide in.'

'Yes,' she agreed, with a sigh. 'I missed that myself. But my father was a wonderful confidant. I could talk to him about things I could never have discussed with my mother. She and I were so unalike it was hard to believe I had any of her genes in me. How did Anna react to Francine's presence?'

'Anna didn't work for me then. After Francine's departure Bethany took over the housekeeping; and did a very good job. But it was a pretty dull life for a girl of seventeen. So I fixed up some digs and a job in London for her. Soon after that Anna came to look after me.'

'I'm afraid she's not going to approve when she comes back and realises that we're sleeping together. Assuming that we still are by the time she's finished convalescing,' she added.

'Have you any reason to doubt that we shall be?' asked David.

'Not at this moment, but who knows? The future is always uncertain. Live for today, that's my motto.'

'A very good one,' he agreed. 'Too many people waste the present by always looking to the future. The here and now is what matters.' He refilled their glasses and raised his in a toast. 'May you live all the days of your life.'

'Is that a quotation?'

'Jonathan Swift.'

Liz lifted her glass. 'May you live all the days of your life,' she echoed.

As she put the glass to her lips, she saw his blue eyes, although still meeting hers, take on the fixed look of someone whose mind has switched to another place, another time.

Instinct told her it was the toast which had triggered a potent memory so that, for a few moments, the past was more real than the present and she had ceased to exist for him.

The blank stare came and went so quickly that if the flight of a swallow had caused her to glance at the sky she would have missed it.

'Does it bother you what Anna thinks?' he asked her.

'Not at all. Well ... perhaps a bit. As she seems to have an exaggeratedly high opinion of me, I'm slightly loath to disillusion her.'

'She won't think badly of you. I shall be blamed for seducing you. But I shouldn't worry about it. It will be some time before she's fit to come back. She'll probably spend several weeks with her daughter in Pisa.'

Anna, when they spent a short time at her bedside the following evening, was pleased to see them, but not up to much conversation. However as the week went on she recovered her normal animation and, now the worst part of the ordeal was safely over, began to enjoy her time in hospital.

One afternoon David asked Liz if she would mind going to Genoa alone. He was expecting a visit from a local builder who was going to estimate the cost of constructing a belvedere in the lower part of the garden. The man should have called that morning, but had telephoned to say he would be delayed.

Since her first time at the wheel, David had encouraged her to drive the Ferrari on several occasions. But always he had been with her. This was the first time she had driven it alone.

Once clear of the twisting coast road, she found it an exhilarating experience to be in control of a sophisticated piece of engineering which had much more in common with the Formula One Grand Prix winners than merely the name and the badge.

In spite of the powerful V8 engine's position in the passenger compartment, and even with the top down, the car was amazingly quiet. She kept the electrically-operated side windows up which blocked out almost all draught and made surging along the *autostrada* at a hundred and twenty kilometres an hour seem no faster than going at sixty in the car she had rented in Spain.

Considering how, with most men, everything to do with motoring seemed to bring out and accentuate all their least likeable macho characteristics, she still found it hard to accept David's totally different attitude.

To him the car wasn't a status symbol or in any way bound up with his sense of virility. It was simply a superb machine which he could afford to own and which gave him pleasure to drive; a pleasure he wanted her to share.

Anna, when she discovered Liz hadn't come in a taxi, but in the Ferrari, threw up her hands in horror. She regarded the car in the light of a dangerous animal and had been apprehensive when Liz had driven her the short distance from the port to the villa.

'It was very wrong of the Signor to make you come here without him. That car goes too fast. It's not safe. One day there will be an accident,' she said, shaking her head.

'He didn't make me come, Anna. I wanted to. I enjoyed the drive. Have they taken your stitches out?'

'*Si*, and you told me truly. It wasn't painful.' The housekeeper began to recount all that had happened to her and the other patients since the previous day.

Eventually, having exhausted that subject, she said, 'You and the Signor, you like each other—*si*?'

'So far we get on very well,' Liz agreed.

'It is time he was married,' said Anna. 'You also, although you are younger, should be thinking of a husband and children.'

Liz needed no reminder. Thoughts of that nature preoccupied her all too easily. She had to make a conscious effort not to daydream on those lines.

She said, her tone carefully casual, 'If the Signor were a marrying man, he would have found a wife by now, don't you think?'

Anna shook her head. 'A wife to suit the Signor isn't easy to find—but perhaps not impossible,' she added, with a meaning look.

Liz foresaw that if she gave Anna the slightest inkling of her feelings, the housekeeper might say something embarrassing to David. The last thing she wanted was for the housekeeper to give him the idea that Liz had marriage in mind. The idea of making their relationship permanent had to emanate from him, because he found their companionship essential to his well-being.

With this in mind, she said, in her most detached tone, 'Artists are different from other people, Anna. Usually their work means more to them than marriage and family responsibilities. Perhaps it's better for painters such as the Signor and myself to create pictures rather than children. The world is becoming too crowded.'

She paused, prepared for a shocked remonstrance, but to her surprise, Anna nodded. 'It's better not to have as many babies as I did. I can remember being glad when I knew I couldn't conceive again. But when there's no shortage of money, to have one child, or two, is good. Without children, who will love and care for us in our old age? To whom shall we leave our savings and the things we treasure?'

Liz refrained from pointing out that many old people did not receive loving care from their offspring.

She said, 'Perhaps when the Signor dies, the Villa Delphini will become a museum. He'll be even more famous by then and people will be interested to see where he lived and worked.'

'It would be better for the villa to become the home of his children and their children. He should have a son to follow him,' Anna said firmly. 'And a pretty daughter. I remember the time when his niece stayed with him. You could see he was fond of her.'

'I believe there was also a Frenchwoman at the villa at that time,' said Liz.

The housekeeper gave her a sharp look. 'Where did you hear that?'

'The Signor told me. He said she was an excellent cook.'

'She was too old for him, too old to give him a son. I used to see them having dinner at Luigi's place. The French one would have married the Signor, if he'd wanted her. You could tell by the way she watched him when he was talking and laughing with the little Signorina. But he didn't want her. A man doesn't marry a woman he can have for nothing.'

A more militant feminist would have been unable to let this last statement pass unargued. But Liz understood the social conditions and pressures which had formed Anna's attitudes.

In her youth, a girl's virginity had been a marketable commodity to be protected by her parents and surrendered only in return for a wedding ring and the lifelong protection it represented. Good women's bodies belonged to their husbands alone. Everything else was a sin and, if known to the world, a disgrace.

Naturally she would regard Francine Valery as a woman without shame—and Liz as well, when she found out what had been happening at the villa in her absence.

'Anna, I have the impression that there may have been some great sadness . . . some kind of tragedy in the Signor's life. Do you know if that is so?' she asked.

'All I know is what I was told by Maria Lipari who used to do some cleaning for him. She said that one day he had to go to England in a hurry because his brother had been killed in an accident. When he came back he brought the Signorina with him. How ill she looked, the poor child! Pale and thin, more like a boy than a girl.'

At this point a priest arrived to visit Anna. After being introduced to him and staying a few minutes more, Liz said it was time for her to leave.

'Take care in that car. Don't drive fast,' was Anna's parting warning.

On the way back Liz mulled over what she had learned. Until now she had assumed it must be a person—a woman—who was responsible for David's bouts of sleeplessness and the other signs that he had some secret heartache.

Perhaps that assumption was off beam. Maybe it was a place.

On his first day at home she had asked him if he had been homesick during his time overseas. With a strange expression on his face, he had admitted he had. But perhaps it wasn't his present home he had missed while thousands of miles away from Europe. Perhaps it was the place in Northamptonshire, Blackmead, he had pined for.

I never go there. My widowed sister-in-law lives there with her two daughters. Margaret and I don't get on. The last time I was at Blackmead was over six years ago.

She remembered him telling her that during lunch at Luigi's. Preoccupied with the powerful attraction he exerted on her, she had let it slip to the back of her mind.

Could it be that, having inherited his brother's estate, the place where they both had grown up, he would have liked to live there, but was prevented from doing so by a strong antagonism between him and the widowed Lady Castle?

What an impossible situation: a family house to which two people, who don't get on, both have a claim, thought Liz.

Naturally Lady Castle would feel entitled to continue living in her late husband's house where, presumably, her daughters had been born. But had she the right to deny David his inheritance? How large a house was Blackmead? Not large enough, it would appear, to be divided into two separate establishments.

Finding her new supposition more acceptable than her previous assumption, Liz took the Rapallo exit and was soon driving up to the villa where a strange car was parked in the forecourt.

It turned out to be the builder's. He was still there, having a glass of wine on the terrace. He was about thirty years old. His father, now semi-retired, had worked for David years before when he had first bought the house. At that time, after standing empty for a year or two, it had needed extensive repairs.

The son, whose name was Toni, shook hands with Liz and gave her a bold black-eyed grin in which she read the conclusion that she was a bit of skirt the Signor had picked up somewhere to share his bed.

She gave him her coolest smile and didn't sit down as she had intended but left them to finish their talk while she went indoors.

A short time later she was rinsing shampoo from her hair under the shower when she heard David enter the bathroom.

'How was Anna?' he asked, raising his voice to be heard above the rush of water.

'She was fine. I shan't be long.'

Liz finished rinsing and turned off the spray while she rubbed in conditioning cream. Before she had finished the shower door opened and David stepped inside with her.

He put his arms round her and said, his lips to her cheek, 'I'm sorry about that bumptious clod. I could have kicked his teeth in for having the gall to leer at you. But if I had, he wouldn't have understood why. He looks at all women like that—all the pretty ones.'

His annoyance soothed her annoyance. She slipped her arms round his waist, delighting in her power to arouse him merely by pressing her wet body to his dry one.

'It doesn't matter, d——' She bit off the endearment which had almost slipped out. Although several times he had called her *carissima*, she had deliberately avoided the use of love-names. 'How was he to know I'm not one of the playgirls who come to places like this, with or without rich protectors?'

'Everything about you is different from those girls. If he can't recognise that, he's more of a fool than I took him for.'

'He's not necessarily stupid. He just hasn't caught up with the new ideas about women. He thinks if I'm living here with you I have to be the type who would do this with him if you didn't have proprietorial rights.'

His arms tightened round her. 'If he thinks that, he can forget about building the belvedere. I don't want him around the place.'

'That's silly, David. If he's the best local builder of

course you must have him. A few undressing looks can't hurt me. He won't do anything.'

'He'd better not try,' he said fiercely.

Liz found herself thrilled by the ring of anger in his voice.

'Forget him,' she whispered, pressing closer.

Later, drying her hair while David went down to fetch a bottle of champagne, it puzzled her that she had liked his display of possessive rage at the thought of Toni looking lecherously at her.

She had been introduced to jealousy by Barney, her first love. For a year she had scarcely dared speak to any other boy at art school. Barney had even been jealous of her girlfriends, her closeness to her father. It had been his irrational jealousy which, once the first attraction had begun to cool, had fouled up their love affair.

She had felt stifled by it, trapped. He was always watching her, suspecting her. Which, as he had been her one and only serious boy-friend, had been wounding as well as irksome.

What David had demonstrated a short time ago had not been unreasonable jealousy, but justifiable anger at another man's boorish behaviour. But how would he have reacted if a more suave type than Toni had paid her eye-compliments, perhaps openly flirted a little? Would David have left it to her to give the man a clear signal she wasn't interested, or would he have started to bristle with possessive fury?

She didn't know. There was so much about him she didn't know. What he was like when he was ill— Richard had been impossible. Whether he ever drank too much. Where he stood on serious issues like capital punishment, nuclear disarmament, the situation in Northern Ireland.

*   *   *

The golden days passed, filled with sunshine, good things to eat, work, wine, laughter and nights of wonderful lovemaking.

How long could this happiness go on? Liz wondered sometimes, as she took a short break from painting to do a few neck and shoulder exercises or to sip a cup of Lapsang Soochong from the flask she made up after breakfast.

Inspired by the many intriguing and beautiful objects David had amassed during his years at the villa, she was painting like mad and turning out some of her best work.

She was looking good, too. Her eyes had an extra sparkle, her skin glowed with health and well-being. She had never felt better in her life.

'Italy seems to suit me,' she told him, one evening, when he had told her she looked ravishing—and this before she had changed to go down to Luigi's.

It was a few minutes to six. He had been working all day, without a break. He had every right to be tired; fit for nothing but an hour's relaxation with a drink and the local newspaper.

Instead he tossed down the last of the wine in his glass and sprang up, reaching for her hands. As he pulled her to her feet, his tall body bent from the waist. Before she knew what was happening, she was hanging over his shoulder, her pigtail dangling, the blood rushing to her head.

'David!' she protested, laughing.

He ignored her appeals to be put down and strode through the house and up the wide time-worn stone staircase.

In the bedroom he let her fall on his side of the great gold bed with enough force to make her gasp although it couldn't have hurt her.

He began to tear off his clothes, his eyes burning slits of blue between narrowed lids.

'Get your clothes off, Liz.' It was a husky command.

Trembling, she fumbled to undo her buttons. She was wearing a white shirt and shorts with a green scarf pulled through the loops on the waistband, and a pair of green-enamelled ear-rings she had bought in a village in Spain.

The shirt was open to the waist, but that was as far as she'd got when David finished stripping off, knelt on the edge of the bed and dived on her like a hawk swooping on its prey.

Perhaps an hour later he stirred in her arms. Raising himself on his elbows, he began to scatter light kisses on her forehead and cheeks. When an ear-ring got in the way of him nibbling her lobe, he carefully removed both hoops and put them on the night table.

'When did you have your ears pierced?' he asked.

'About ten years ago when I started taking an interest in antique jewels. Maddeningly, nowadays, a lot of jewellers take the original hooks off old ear-rings and replace them with modern fittings which I think spoils them.'

'With your lovely neck you can wear the long dangly ones,' he said, running his fingertips over the shape of her chin and the sweeping lines of her throat.

'I have a pair like that with me. They're antique paste, bought in Spain. I found them in a most unlikely little jeweller's shop. But they're not really suitable to wear for dinner at Luigi's.'

'Are you getting sick of Luigi's? Would you like to go up to the hotel where you can wear the ear-rings?'

Liz shook her head, smiling. 'I love Luigi's.'

They lay, making lazy pillow talk, David's touch

feather-light on her collarbones and the golden-brown curves of her shoulders.

'Somewhere I have a ruby which should fit your navel,' he murmured, having shifted lower down the bed to lie with his head on her breasts. 'Or would you prefer an amethyst?'

'I think I should really prefer an aquamarine. One of those deep blue-green stones like a chunk of crystallised sea-water,' she replied in a dreamy tone, stroking his thick hair. 'What a pity men don't wear jewels any more.'

'Some of them do. Gold medallions.'

'Yuck!' said Liz, with distaste. 'But you would look splendid with a pair of gold armlets and one of those beaten gold collars the ancient Phoenicians used to wear. Or was it the Thracians? No, but seriously, you would,' she insisted, feeling him shaking with laughter. 'Not to wear in public, of course, only in private with me. You have a wonderful torso. It makes me wish I could sculpt.'

David turned over on to his forearms. 'I've been thinking about your suggestion that we should paint each other in bed. A better idea would be for me to paint you. Would you mind posing for a full-length nude portrait?'

'Why should I mind when I spend half my time in the nude?'

'If it turned out well—and I'm not a portraitist, remember—I should want to include the picture in my next show in London. You may not care for the prospect of the world and his wife gawking at all this luscious flesh,' he said, with a sweeping survey of her body. 'It would be bound to cause comment about our relationship. You may feel that wouldn't be good for your professional reputation.'

She touched the hard slant of his cheekbone and the deep laughter-line down his cheek.

'I'd count it an honour to be painted by the great David Warren,' she told him softly. 'But there is one condition.'

'Which is?'

She gave him a glinting smile. 'That before every sitting you make love to me.'

'I have every intention of doing that. There's about half an hour, perhaps less, when you have a special look. That's what I want to catch.'

'What sort of look?' asked Liz, not sure if he were serious.

'I can't put it into words, but I think I might get it on canvas.'

He leaned closer and started to kiss her; soft, subtle kisses like the slow opening and closing of a sea anemone.

When Liz came to the end of her book about Casimir, the ship's cat, she showed it to David. He spent a silent twenty minutes reading the text and studying the illustrations based on sketches of Portofino's many cats made while she was living in the port.

At last he said, 'It's a delightful book, Liz. I believe you could have a huge success with it. You can't trust this to the mail. You must take it to your agent in person. Let's fly to London tomorrow. I have some things to do there. We can stay a couple of nights. I'll call the airport.'

She said, 'Unless you have something urgent to do in London, I don't think I need rush this over as quickly as that.'

It was not that she wasn't impatient to hear her agent's reaction. She had an instinctive feeling that, if once they broke the spell of this summer idyll, they might never recapture it. Away from the Villa Delphini, in another environment, they might both see each other in a different and less flattering light.

'Certainly you must. We've both been sequestered too long. We need to find out what's going on where the action is,' he said firmly.

'But you've only just come back from a long time away. Surely you aren't bored already?' she protested, with a thrust of anxiety.

If he were bored, was it, in part, with her?

'Parts of Australia were fascinating, but I didn't find Sydney as stimulating as New York or London or even Toronto,' said David. 'Nor do a lot of Australians. Germaine Greer, for example. Having established an international reputation, the *dottoresa* didn't hare back to her homeland. She bought a summer house in Tuscany, sensible woman, and commutes between Europe and America.'

'Do you *like* Germaine Greer?' she asked, startled.

'I think she's tremendous fun. Not afraid to be her own woman. I think she could lay off the four-letter words with advantage, but otherwise—yes, I like her. You must have read *The Obstacle Race*, her book about women painters, haven't you?'

'No, I haven't. Somehow I missed it.'

'I'll get you a copy in London. You'll find it fascinating.'

'I can't believe that you *like* her. Most men go purple and swell up if one mentions her name.'

'They're the ones who are nervous of women with power and influence. The women who frighten me are the ones who can't stand on their own feet. I prefer achievers.'

Perhaps because they were more easily sent packing when the party was over, thought Liz, with a hollow feeling.

David booked them on an early flight and rang up a hotel in London to reserve a room.

'I hope that's okay with you,' he said, when the call

was over. 'I usually put up at the Cavendish. It's not the Savoy or the Ritz, but it's convenient and comfortable for a short visit. I should have consulted you first,' he added, with a twinkle. 'Sorry about that. The habit of taking the initiative in matters of that sort dies hard.'

'I don't mind in the least,' she assured him. 'I don't know any hotels in London, as far as staying in them goes. I've been wined and dined at a few. Listen, David, I'm absolutely *not* going to let you pay for this jaunt. If you won't agree to split the expenses down the middle, I——'

She had meant to say 'I won't go', but changed to, 'I shan't come back.'

He gave her a thoughtful look. Perhaps it lasted five seconds. It seemed to her like five minutes.

Oh, my goodness, I've blown it, she thought. He's going to say, *Well, perhaps it might be better if you didn't. All good things have to come to an end . . .*

David said, 'All right, we'll share the expenses. Would you rather have a separate room? I can easily ring back and ask them to keep me a single room on another floor. That way only the maid will know you haven't slept by yourself.'

Relief flooded through her. 'I don't mind who knows we're close friends. Separate rooms would be silly . . . a waste of money. I just want to pay my way.'

They were in central London by noon. While they were unpacking, David suggested they had lunch at the Overseas League where the buttery had a view across Green Park.

As they walked along Jermyn Street, past windows displaying striped poplins for men's bespoke shirts, Liz began to recapture the excitement of her first months in London as a young student. In those days she couldn't afford to buy any of the lovely temptations in the shop windows; only to gaze and admire, and to educate her taste for the day when she would have some money to spare.

The League, of which David was a member, was housed in a former mansion at the end of a cul-de-sac off St James's Street, the home of several of London's most famous men's clubs.

Inside, the building was much the way she imagined the interiors of the clubs. There was a porters' desk, a thickly carpeted inner lobby giving a glimpse of the ornately plastered room which was now the buttery, and then a few stairs leading up to a large inner entrance hall with pillars and a grand staircase balustraded with wrought-iron and with an Oriental screen on the half-landing.

'Being in England, I'm going to drink beer. How about you?' David asked. 'Gin and tonic?'

Liz nodded. 'That would be fine.'

The other people in the bar were not conspicuously elegant. The men's suits had the recognisable look of good cloth and good cut which has stood up to many years' wear. It was how her father had dressed. The women matched them in vintage Jaeger with good if uninteresting bags. But there was one girl on a bar stool who caught Liz's clothes-loving eye and made her impatient to browse in her favourite shops. She was still wearing the raw umber flying suit she had travelled in. David was equally casual in an Italian sweater and pale khaki pants. But she had seen a suit go into his travel bag and, later, she meant to show him how she could look when she put her mind to it.

She watched him chatting to the steward behind the bar, his face and hands strikingly bronzed in a room full of people who had not been enjoying a hot summer. Today, so the taxi driver had told them, was the first sunny day after three weeks of showery weather.

'The best view in London,' said David, when he returned to their table. 'This is actually better than the Ritz view because here we're further away from the noise of Piccadilly.'

He shifted his chair, the better to look through the window at the trees and grass slopes of the park beyond the League's garden. She wondered if it made him think of the grounds at Blackmead, and if to be back in England was, in part, a painful experience.

An hour later they went separate ways; David on foot to the art galleries in the area and Liz in a cab to Knightsbridge which she preferred to Mayfair for clothes shopping.

It was the night when Harrods and the shops in Sloane Street stayed open later than usual. She didn't get back to the hotel until after six.

She expected to find David waiting for her. However when, laden with parcels, she fed the key-card into the slot and pushed open the door, their bedroom was empty. But there was a package on the bed and a note in his handwriting.

Meeting old friend for drink after work. Back by 7 p.m. Unable to get decent seats for either of the plays we wanted, but have booked good seats for tomorrow and a table for dinner tonight.

It was signed *D*, followed by six small crosses and one large one representing seven kisses.

The parcel contained *The Obstacle Race*. She was tempted to dip into it, then realised she hadn't time. It would take all of forty-five minutes to get ready.

The bedroom had a refrigerator stocked with a variety of drinks including half bottles of champagne. She opened one and took it to the bathroom with her. She ran the taps, tried the champagne, took off her clothes, drank some more and began to cream off her make-up.

Ten minutes later, after a refreshing soak, she stepped on to the bathmat and reached for a towel. Between them, the bath and the bubbly had banished the feeling of tiredness induced by being in a big city, surrounded by people and traffic, after the peace of Portofino.

Not that she hadn't enjoyed the afternoon. It had been a long time since she had shopped with the added pleasure of expecting to light up a man's eyes.

At two minutes past seven David returned. By then she was sitting in a chair, debating whether to open the other half bottle. She had been ready only a few minutes.

The first thing he said, as he was closing the door, was, 'You've bought some new scent.'

Liz rose from the chair, the supple honey-coloured folds of her new Jean Muir flowing from her shoulders to brush the slim curves of her figure with the timeless chic which had made the British designer's clothes loved and collected by discerning women all over the world.

The night before she had shut herself in her bathroom to colour her hair, a process which always left it silky and sheeny. Now coiled and twisted, and pinned up, it gave her a sophistication David had never seen before.

'My God! You look stunning, Liz.'

'Thank you. The scent is *Chamade*. I thought you might be getting bored with *Shalimar*.'

'Nothing about you could bore me.' He crossed the room and took her hands, kissing them both on the backs and then turning them over, pressing his lips into her palms. 'I'll kiss you properly later. Right now, looking like that, I'm sure you don't want to be hugged. Anyway, I must get showered. I should think I reek of cigarette smoke. I've been in a bar full of smokers.'

Since they had parted, he had put on a tan blouson of very fine Italian leather, almost as supple as the stuff of her dress. Having taken it off, he felt in an inside pocket and produced a flat leather case.

'I nearly forgot. I saw something I thought you'd like. If you don't, I can change it.'

He opened the case and showed her an antique bracelet made of very finely carved cameos with a pair of drop ear-rings to match. Set in gold, between delicate links, each cameo depicted a classical head, some in half, some in three-quarter profile.

Liz's interest in antique jewels had made her able to appreciate the unusual quality of the set, and to have an approximate idea what he must have paid for it.

She was taken aback by such an exquisite and costly present when all she had bought for him was a linen sports shirt in a particularly pleasing shade of pale terracotta.

'David . . . it's perfectly beautiful . . . but much, *much* too extravagant!' she exclaimed.

He put the case on the dressing counter and picked up the bracelet to clasp it around her left wrist.

'I was looking for an aquamarine, but the ones I was shown were too pale. There was nothing the colour of sea-water.'

Remembering the conversation he was alluding to, she said, 'David, I was only joking. It wasn't a hint.' Regardless of what might happen to her evening make-up, she put her arms round his neck. 'I'm a free gift, as they say in the ads. No strings. No expectations.'

He put his hands lightly on her waist. 'I know that, beautiful girl, but surely we can give each other presents sometimes. Are you never going to buy me an unbirthday present?' he asked, with a mock-doleful grimace.

'Of course . . . as I did today. But it's only a shirt, nothing as madly lavish as these divine cameos. Thank you, my . . . dear friend.' She reached up and kissed him, not caring if it smudged the pencilled outline, lipstick and lip-gloss she had applied with such care a short time before.

She had almost called him 'my darling', she realised later, when he had gone to shower and she was removing the pearl studs she had been wearing.

There hadn't been time that afternoon to go to her bank and get out some of her good jewellery. The studs were from Harvey Nichols, her favourite store for accessories and costume jewellery. She had bought them a few hours earlier, with a single strand of inexpensive creamy pearls to lie close to the base of her throat.

In the bank she had a string of cultured pearls sent to her by her mother for her twenty-first birthday.

'*A thirty-inch string of eight-millimetre matched pearls is basic to every woman's jewel case,*' Mrs Eugene P. Thornwell of Boston had written to her daughter.

At that time, influenced by Zandra Rhodes, an ascending star of British design, Liz had been dyeing her hair lilac and dressing with zany panache in clothes bought from junk shops. The pearls, symbolic of her mother's religious devotion to conventional good taste, had been the most boring present she had received.

But a few years later, as her taste had matured, she had begun to enjoy them, and to wear them more and more often with the silk shirts and well-tailored pants which gradually replaced the deliberate eccentricites of her student days.

Now, as she put on the cameo ear-rings and surveyed her reflection, she realised that this evening, in appearance, she looked a person of whom even her mother would approve.

What Mrs Thornwell would not find easy to tolerate was Liz's relationship with David. With few exceptions, all the daughters of her friends had made socially suitable marriages soon after leaving college. And if many of them were now divorced, or patching over the first cracks, Mrs Thornwell would find that preferable to having a daughter of twenty-eight who was still single and living with a lover.

Not that she was likely to find out because, in their twice-yearly exchange of letters, Liz never referred to her private life, only to her professional activities, something which Mrs Thornwell could speak of with pride when the women who shared her good works asked after her daughter in England.

'Where are we dining?' she asked, when David came out of the bathroom, vigorously towelling his wet hair.

'I thought we'd try Le Gavroche.'

'That's the place in Sloane Street, isn't it?'

'Used to be, when the brothers Roux first opened it. Now it's in Upper Brook Street near the American Embassy. May I borrow your drier?'

She produced her small hairdrier for him.

As he plugged it in, David said, 'It'll be interesting to see what we think of the place. Michelin gave it a third star not long ago, which some people might say was the French applauding French cuisine.'

His method of drying his hair proved, if proof were necessary, how little vanity there was in him. Using the drier at full speed, not even bothering to watch himself in the mirror, he applied the current of hot air while raking his hair with his fingers. When it was almost dry, he brushed it back smoothly from his forehead and temples, then quickly combed in his parting.

'Would you like a drink while you're waiting?' He opened the fridge and took out the other half bottle.

They shared it while he finished dressing. In a well-cut grey suit and beige shirt, with a pink and beige tie, his tall figure had an authority which hadn't struck her before, or not as forcibly.

Casually dressed at Portofino, and even earlier today in his comfortable travelling clothes, he had not looked quite as he did now. The formal clothes played down his physique, hiding the powerful body under the fine wool cloth. But they played up something seigneurial which she hadn't noticed before. Not that it should have surprised her. The fact that he was a younger son who had chosen to make his own way in the world couldn't alter the inborn assurance inherited from generations of English landowners.

Suddenly, looking at David as he strapped on his watch and picked up his wallet and loose change, she felt she was seeing another man; not David Warren, the artist, but his alter ego, Sir David Castle, who, if ever he was able to return to Blackmead, would have no place in his life for her.

It was a curious illusion and one which, for an instant, sent a premonitory shiver through her.

Then he smiled at her. 'Ready to go?'

The warm, blue-eyed smile made nonsense of the idea that he was two people; the passionate lover of Portofino, and another man, almost a stranger.

Presently, strolling leisurely along Bond Street, pausing to look in the windows of Maud Frizon, Chanel and Asprey's, Liz forgot her momentary disquiet.

At Brook Street they turned the corner and headed for the green gardens of Grosvenor Square, a few blocks ahead. They were passing Claridges Hotel when a man came out of the main entrance and said loudly, 'David . . . what a surprise!'

'Oh, hello, Miles,' David answered.

'Haven't seen you in years, my dear chap. How are you? No need to ask. As fit as a fiddle, by the look of you.' He paused, looking at Liz, including her in his smile.

He was probably the same age as David but, being overweight with rather bloodshot brown eyes, he looked considerably older.

'Liz, this is Miles Dacre. His father and mine were near neighbours. Miss Redwood is a fellow artist.'

'How do you do, Miss Redwood. I surmise, from your admirable sun-tan, that you also live in Italy, like this fortunate fellow.'

'At the moment, yes,' she agreed.

'How I envy you both! It's been a shocking year here. But you seem to have brought the sun with you. How long are you staying?' He addressed David.

After a few minutes' small talk, they said goodbye and walked on.

'Now he'll have something interesting to tell his wife when he goes home,' David said drily. 'Who do you think I ran into in London, Elizabeth? Castle's rotter of a brother. Had a damned good-looking girl with him.'

It was a good imitation of Miles Dacre's voice and manner which made her laugh.

A few steps further on, she said, 'Why should he call you a rotter?'

She looked up at his face as she asked. His expression changed only fractionally, yet intuition told her it had been a slip of the tongue which he regretted.

'Miles is a farmer,' he answered. 'A bit of a clod

intellectually. He regards all artists as rotters—unless they're feminine and pretty.'

She could believe the truth of that. Even in the short time they had spent with Mr Dacre, she had formed the impression that he was a male counterpart of her mother, a man of conventional outlook with no time for those he regarded as outsiders.

At the same time she didn't think David's reply was the whole truth. There had to be some other reason why Miles might use that expression when reporting the encounter to his wife.

Suddenly she remembered David explaining his single status by telling her that, as a young man, he had loved another man's wife. Perhaps his infatuation had been noticed and talked about. But even if it had, he wouldn't have been branded a rotter by local society unless he had actually been known to commit adultery with her. Or unless——

Her train of thought was interrupted when David gripped her arm above the elbow and jerked her backwards. Liz came out of her abstracted state to find she had been on the point of stepping off the kerb into the path of a speeding taxi.

'I hope you don't cross roads like that when you're by yourself,' he said, somewhat curtly.

'I'm sorry. I wasn't thinking.'

'You were thinking, but not about crossing the road.' He looked searchingly down at her. 'What was on your mind?'

'I ... was wondering about Elizabeth Dacre ... what sort of woman she is?'

Would he believe her? she wondered.

It seemed that he did. He said, 'Horsey. Does her hair with a curry-comb by the look of it and has a backside as big as her horses' hindquarters.'

Liz didn't laugh. Her best friend at art school had

been a potentially lovely but overweight girl whose youth had been blighted by the kind of metabolism which made slimming a punishment.

'Poor thing,' she said sympathetically.

'Poor Miles,' was David's comment. 'It must be like going to bed with one of his prize sows.'

'David, that's cruel,' she objected. 'It's not like you to be unkind.'

He looked down at her, something puzzling in his expression.

'You're never beastly, are you? Your nature's as nice as your face. I might look benign, but I'm not. Life is too short to be wasted on fools, bores and women who, as the French say, make no effort to arrange themselves.'

'Anna doesn't arrange herself, and you've "wasted" a lot of time with her since she went into hospital.'

'Anna's no fool and she amuses me. Although some women of her age can be attractive to older men, she's not that kind. She's quite right not to let her daughter persuade her to have her hair permed. It wouldn't suit her. Life has been pretty brutal to her. Physically she's ten years older than an American widow of the same age. But it's given her a kind of beauty I don't see in blue-rinsed matrons in Crimplene trouser suits. Her beauty is like an old olive tree or a stone stair worn down by being climbed for hundreds of years. You see faces exactly like hers in the crowd scenes of the great masters.'

Liz murmured agreement before lapsing into silence. Her mind was still reeling from the flash of illumination which, but for David's swift action, might have caused her to be hit by the taxi.

Seen in this new clear light, her theories about his secret unhappiness had suddenly fitted together like a jigsaw puzzle after several missing pieces are found to have dropped on the floor or be still in the box.

What she had not seen before was the correlation between his youthful passion for another man's wife and his reasons for staying away from his ancestral home.

When he had told her that he and his late brother's wife didn't get on, he must have been telling a white lie to cover the fact that she was the woman whom he had loved, and still did.

That would explain everything. Loving her, he could never ask her to leave Blackmead. But neither could he live there with her, even in separate quarters. It could only serve to reactivate a pain which his exile had not cured, but had at least dulled.

Poor David, she thought with compassion.

And poor me, was her next thought.

CHAPTER FOUR

LATER, looking back on that evening, Liz had no recollection of entering the restaurant or being shown to the table reserved for them.

She must have acted normally or David would have made some comment; asked her what was the matter. But although some small part of her mind had remained in control of her physical behaviour, most of it had been blanked out by the shattering realisation of what it meant to be deeply in love with a man who could never be hers in the fullest sense.

By the time she had recovered her wits, they were seated at a banquette table near the centre of the restaurant, drinking sherry and studying the *carte*.

By a strong exercise of will Liz forced herself to concentrate on choosing what to eat. But she was relieved when the decisions were made and she could relax. In her present state of mind, choosing between *Papillote de saumon fumé Claudine* and *Oeufs froids Carême* was too much of a mental effort. Like someone in shock, she needed to rest and recover.

She had taken it for granted that David would select the wines. She was dismayed when he said to the waiter, 'May we have another wine list for my guest, please?'

'Certainly, sir.' The man produced one and handed it to her. 'Madame.'

'Thank you.' She took it, but said, 'David, I'm perfectly happy to drink whatever you choose.'

He arched an eyebrow. 'That's not an attitude Steinam and Greer would approve of.'

'Maybe not, but it's every woman's inalienable right to be a clinging vine sometimes. It probably won't last through dinner, but the vine mood is on me now, so make the most of it.'

As he grinned at her, she went on, 'Actually, having spent a chunk of my life with a man whose *amour propre* was heavily dependent on playing the winesmanship game, I haven't had much opportunity to develop my own judgment.'

Her references to Richard was deliberate, a kind of defensive reaction to this new situation of being no longer able to delude herself that she wasn't in line for heartbreak. But at least she didn't have to reveal her frightening vulnerability to David. Indeed she must do just the opposite: try to seem harder than she was.

She could tell that he thought her reference to her previous lover to be in questionable taste. As indeed it had been. His face stiffened as it would at a racist remark or a risqué joke which was vulgar rather than witty.

He said coldly, 'Then I suggest you make use of your present opportunity.'

It was a deserved put-down, but it hurt her far more than he could have intended. As, obediently, she opened the wine list, she was appalled to find her eyes smarting. Through a blur of tears she looked at the impressive list of French and German wines.

Presently, in the first moment when there was no one attending to them, David reached for her hand and squeezed it.

'Forgive me, Liz,' he said, in a low voice. 'That was a swinish thing to say. Whenever I think of that guy who made you unhappy . . . But that's no reason to lash out at *you*, is it, sweet?'

Regardless of who might be watching, he brushed his lips over her knuckles, his blue eyes contrite.

The tenderness of his apology almost had her in floods. But although her mouth trembled, she managed to blink back the tears.

Fortunately at this point their soufflé arrived, with a covered basket of freshly made hot Melba toast.

'It was Albert and Michel Roux who brought *nouvelle cuisine* to England; or at any rate were pre-eminent in launching the new style of cooking on this side of the Channel,' said David, while they were eating the vegetable-filled soufflé. 'I've long preferred it to classic French cooking, but bad *nouvelle* is atrocious and there's a lot of it about.'

For the first time since their arrival Liz began to pay attention to their surroundings.

The décor was mainly in a subdued darkish green. The most striking feature of it was the use of long strips of bamboo to outline the edges of the walls and alcoves.

'I wonder who the designer was?' she said, recognising the hand of a top professional in the cohesive style of the restaurant's appointments.

'David Mlinaric. He took over as adviser to the National Trust after John Fowler died. If ever I ... I've seen one or two of the houses he's done for private clients. I like his style very much.'

She could guess the rest of what he had started to say. *If ever I go back to Blackmead and want a room re-designed I should choose him to do it.*

For the next course they had both chosen the *papillote* of smoked salmon. When it came, she couldn't remember seeing a more enticing presentation than the aspic-glistening parcel of coral pink salmon garnished with a diamond composed of two small black diamonds joined to two small white ones, which she took to be slivers of black and white truffle.

A few moments later she discovered that inside the

outer wrapping of paper-thin salmon was a very rich purée of salmon, smoked trout and cream. Eaten with the brittle, crunchy toast and accompanied by the wine they had chosen, it was a memorable experience.

While they were enjoying it, she noticed a man in the uniform of a chef, but without the tall toque on his dark head, going round the tables greeting people. He had the quality called 'presence' and a face and manner which would make him attractive to women, she thought, as she watched him circulate.

'Is that one of the Roux brothers, do you think?' she murmured to David.

'Yes, that's Albert Roux.'

'How do you know? I thought you hadn't been here before?'

'I haven't. But both of them are well-known faces to anyone interested in gastronomy. Michel was given the title *Meilleur Ouvrier de France* by President Giscard d'Estaing. Albert started his career as a commis chef for Lady Astor, Britain's first woman M.P. He also cooked at the French Embassy in London and the British Embassy in Paris.'

Perhaps it was part of being a great chef-restaurateur to know if your patrons were notable people in their fields.

When, a few moments after their empty plates had been whisked away, the Frenchman approached their table, he said, 'Good evening, Mr Warren. I am an admirer of your paintings. It's a pleasure to welcome you to Le Gavroche.'

David rose to shake hands with him. 'And to be here, Monsieur Roux. This is Miss Redwood, a talented colleague of mine.'

'*Enchanté, mademoiselle.*' The famous chef bowed over her hand with Gallic aplomb, his dark eyes admiring.

He stayed chatting for a few minutes before moving away to another table where, she observed, his place of honour in his profession was not accorded the tribute which David had paid him when he rose to his feet.

His good manners were part of his charm for her. She had frequently cringed at Richard's cavalier attitude to people who waited on him in restaurants and shops. In the early days of their relationship, she had been sufficiently infatuated to try not to notice his lapses. Deep down she had always known that if her father had met Richard he would have thought, if not said, that he was 'a bit of a bounder'.

Had he met David, she knew, he would have approved of him, not because they had both been born into what people called 'the old boy network', but because it was David's nature as much as his upbringing which made him look at waiters and see them as people not as mere automata, which had been Richard's attitude.

After the richness of the *papillote* they were brought a champagne sorbet to refresh their palates.

'David, I didn't thank you for *The Obstacle Race*,' she exclaimed. 'It was thoughtful of you to remember I wanted to read it.'

'Don't count on starting to read it in bed tonight,' he said, with a teasing glance. 'I have other plans for you, *carissima*.'

The sorbet was followed by the main course; a fan of duck breast arranged over a leek and spinach sauce and garnished with pieces of mange-tout peas and chopped chives.

'What time are you seeing your agent tomorrow?' asked David.

'We're going to have lunch together. What are your plans for the day?'

'I thought I'd see the exhibition at the Royal

Academy. Care to come with me? Or would you rather go shopping?'

'I've done all my shopping. I'd love to come with you. And in the afternoon?'

'At two I'm having my teeth checked, but that won't take long. By half-past two I'll be free. What time do you expect your lunch to be over?'

'Not late. Jane has a busy afternoon. I should think I'll be free about the same time as you.'

When they left Le Gavroche, replete after a pudding of raspberries sandwiched between layers of sweet, buttery biscuit, they both felt like more exercise.

Arms linked, fingers intertwined, they strolled round the other side of the Square towards Carlos Place.

'My parents always stayed there when they came to London,' said David, with a nod at the Edwardian façade of the Connaught Hotel.

And he must have stayed there with them on occasions, thought Liz, knowing the Connaught was a home away from home for many upper-crust English families who wouldn't be seen dead in such ostentatiously opulent palaces as the Dorchester and Grosvenor House. But now he stays at the Cavendish. Is that a matter of expense? Or because I am with him?

'If I were still a member of Annabel's, we could dance,' he said, in Berkeley Square. 'I haven't been in there for ... God, it must be getting on for twenty years. Some of the young things dancing in there tonight weren't born when I was last there.'

His tone was cheerful. Evidently the exclusive club held no poignant memories for him. He had never been there with his sister-in-law, watching her dance with her husband and longing to hold her in his arms.

The lights of the Ritz Casino beckoned from Piccadilly as they walked along Berkeley Street.

'Aren't you excited about tomorrow? Showing Casimir to your agent?' he asked, looking down at her.

Liz agreed that she was. But in fact the future of her book seemed a trivial thing now compared with the outcome of her love for David.

When they arrived at their room, the curtains had been drawn and the bedclothes turned down.

She said, 'It was a delicious meal. Thank you for taking me there.'

'Thank you for giving me the pleasure of having the best-looking, best-dressed woman in the restaurant at my table.' He took her lightly in his arms. 'You look a little tired now. It's been a long crowded day. If you want to fall into bed with your new book, go ahead.'

His tender consideration pierced her to the heart. Hiding her face against his shoulder, she murmured, 'You're very nice to me, David.'

'If I weren't, you'd be off. One has to watch one's step with you independent females,' he said quizzically.

But I'm not independent any more, was her unspoken answer. I need you in my life. I can't be happy without you.

'I'm going to see if there's anything worth watching on TV,' he went on, as he released her.

While he tried different channels, Liz took first turn in the bathroom. Her shopping spree had included an extravagantly glamorous nightdress and peignoir imported from Paris. The robe, with its hand-smocked yoke fanning into soft flowing folds of palest almond-green voile and its full sleeves caught at the wrists with more delicate smocking, was almost demure. The matching nightdress was not. It had a white lace top cut to cling to her breasts, veiling them in a way which was deliberately seductive. She knew that if David saw her in it, he would immediately want to take it off. That was the point of the nightdress.

When she returned to the bedroom, David was slowly undressing while watching a panel of politicians discussing the latest crisis in world affairs.

He glanced at her, noting the new robe. 'That's pretty.'

'Thank you.'

She had washed her bra, briefs and tights and hung them to dry in the bathroom. Now she hung up the Jean Muir dress and put away her slip, shoes and bag.

His attention was on the screen when she took off the robe and climbed into bed, propping *The Obstacle Race* against her raised knees. When the programme presenter wound up the discussion, David went to the bathroom, but he didn't turn off the set. Liz was vaguely aware of the MGM lion roaring to introduce a movie, but she was more interested in reading the introductory chapter of Germaine Greer's book.

'I'm going to have a nightcap. How about you, sweet?'

She looked up to see David taking a one-drink-size bottle of Martell from the fridge.

She nodded. 'Yes, please.'

She hadn't known he possessed a pair of pyjamas. He had never worn them at the villa. Tonight he was wearing the trousers, but not the jacket, of a pair he must keep in reserve for staying at hotels.

Although he wasn't a vain man, the artist in him made him choose his clothes with a discriminating eye for design and colour. The pyjama pants were silk with a small geometric pattern in navy and white.

A few moments later there was a glass of brandy on each of the night tables and he was in bed beside her, settling his bare brown torso against the pillowed headboard.

The film was an old one; a World War Two love story with tragedy looming. From time to time as she sipped her brandy, Liz glanced at the screen and then returned to the book. Since her teens she had had a secret weakness for tear-jerkers. This was one she had missed. Gradually the story unfolding on the television compelled her to stop reading and watch.

Had she been alone, during the closing scenes when the girl had received the news that her lover had been killed and was reading his final letter in a voice-over sequence. she would have wept unrestrainedly. With David beside her she had to repress her emotions, biting her lips to stop them trembling, her throat thick with unshed tears.

When the film came to an end, David switched off the set from the bedside control panel and said he was going to brush his teeth.

As soon as the bathroom door closed, Liz's control broke down. Snatching a handful of tissues from the box on her night table, she held them against her face, her slim shoulders shaking with the sobs she could no longer contain.

She knew why the film had upset her. She had seen, in the girl's stricken face, her own feelings when the time came for her and David to part. As come it must if he could never love her.

He came back sooner than she expected, before she had regained control. Praying he wouldn't catch sight of her face, she scrambled out of bed and bolted for the bathroom.

'Liz!' He stepped in her path and caught her by the upper arms. 'Liz, what's the matter?'

'Nothing ... nothing ... I want to go to the loo.' The words came out in strangled gasps.

'You've been crying.' He drew her against him.

'It was s-such a s-sad film.'

To her horror the floodgates reopened. With no tissues to staunch them, her tears spurted on to his chest. It was impossible to stop them. This second bout of weeping was worse than the first. She felt that her heart was breaking for all the girls in real life whose men had been killed in a war, and on her own account.

David held her close and let her cry. When her sobbing slackened a little, he picked her up and carried her to her side of the bed. He sat down with her on his lap and reached for some tissues to give her.

She took them gratefully, mopping her cheeks and his wet chest.

'I'm terribly sorry,' she whispered unsteadily. 'I should never have watched that film. I'm the world's worst weeper at sad films!'

'No need to apologise, *carissima*. I had a lump in my throat a couple of times.'

'You didn't *dissolve*,' she muttered. 'My face must look like a stewed plum.'

'Let's see.' He tilted it up. 'No, it doesn't at all. You look like a little girl who's lost her teddy bear . . . your eyelashes all stuck together and your cheeks pink and shiny.' His gaze moved to her parted lips. 'Only little girls don't have beautiful Botticelli mouths.' Very gently, very lightly, he kissed it.

'Oh, David . . ' She flung her arms round his neck. 'Oh, David, I——'

I love you so much. Please, please, can't you try to love me?

But of course she could never say that to him. Love was a spontaneous condition. It couldn't be bought or begged, or in any way forced into existence. She could only wait and hope.

She said, 'What's a Botticelli mouth?'

'Didn't you ever study Botticelli's paintings? All those lovely girls dancing barefoot have a little in-curve in the centre of their lower lips ... like this one of yours.' He touched it with his fingertip. 'It was one of the first things I noticed about you.'

'The first things I noticed about you were your bristly chin and your shoulders,' she said, re-membering the first fraught moments when he had been a stranger in her bed.

'I haven't seen this before, have I?'

His finger had moved from her mouth to touch the fine clinging lace at the top of her nightgown.

As she shook her head, he began to investigate the bow of pale green rouleaux on her shoulder to find out if it were stitched in place or would come undone.

The bow itself didn't unfasten, but it did hide a loop and a knot which came apart. With both knots released, carefully he unpeeled the lace and bent his lips to the valley between her bared breasts.

Liz closed her eyes, relaxing against his supporting arm. Exhausted by the storm of tears, she was doubtful that she could respond. Yet a few moments later the touch of his warm lips and hands had quickened the first thrilling tremors.

As she gave a faint murmur of pleasure, his touch became firmer, his lips more insistent. Soon she was stretched on the bed, nightdress removed, her slim body stretched like a sacrifice as slowly, with patience and skill, he coaxed her senses to life.

Occasionally, in between her statutory Christmas and birthday letters, Mrs Eugene P. Thornwell of Cambridge, Massachusetts, would write a note to her daughter asking Liz to be helpful to Americans visiting London.

Usually this would result in Liz meeting them for a drink at whichever hotel they were staying at, to be quizzed about the best places to buy cashmeres, English walking shoes, tweeds and anything else 'typically British'.

The least expensive cashmeres in London were to be found at Marks & Spencer, although, as Liz would point out, the styling might not appeal to them, American women tending to prefer short-waisted sweaters to the hip-length style which was standard at the famous Marble Arch branch of the store.

To help them avoid buying clothes there which were one size too small, she would let them into a secret known to many experienced London shoppers. Directly opposite the store was the comfortable Selfridges Hotel where, in the first floor powder room, hosts of women, including herself, had tried on the clothes they had just bought at Marks & Spencer to make sure they fitted.

In Liz's case, she usually 'paid' for her use of the cloakroom by having coffee in the lounge, or lunch in the apple green restaurant called The Picnic Basket.

This was where, the next day, she met her agent, Jane Cobb Adams. After lunch Jane wanted to dash across the street and stock up on what she still called pantyhose.

She was an American whose second husband was an English architect. She had tremendous vitality and managed to combine being a wife, mother, hostess and agent without apparent effort. But she had confided to Liz that sometimes she suffered from prostrating migraines after a period of extra-hectic activity.

'But I guess that's a small price to pay for "having it all",' she had said, on that occasion, quoting the title of a book she had lent Liz. 'Although I wouldn't agree with that when I'm having one,' she had added.

'You've never had migraine? Be grateful. It's the most terrible pain. I'd sooner be in labour any day!'

Jane's first words when they met for lunch were, 'What happened to you? You look great. Don't tell me, let me guess. You've stopped being an unpaid dogsbody to that selfish slob Richard.'

Liz nodded.

'Not a moment too soon,' Jane said crisply. 'That's the best news I've heard this month. Just as long as you're not so in love with your new guy that you let *him* walk roughshod over you.'

'What makes you think there's someone new in my life?'

'Am I wrong?'

This time Liz shook her head.

'Where did you meet him?' asked Jane. 'In Italy, I presume? Thanks for the postcards, but a letter would have been better. I've been worried about you. To tell you the truth, I knew you and Richard had split. He called me and told me.'

'Really? What did he say?' asked Liz, with only mild curiosity.

'He said would I come round right away and get all your things packed and stored.'

'Jane, he didn't! How could he?' Liz fumed, in a sudden uprush of anger. 'He knew perfectly well our cleaning woman, Mrs Lewis, could have handled that. I wrote to her listing the things she might not have known belonged to me—books and cassettes, things like that. He had no right to bother you. I suppose he was furious with me and thought making a nuisance of himself to one of my friends would be a petty revenge. I don't know what I ever saw in him,' she admitted, with chagrin. 'And yet at one time he seemed . . .' She left the sentence unfinished, unwilling to dwell on that disillusionment.

'I can say the same about Bob, my first husband. Most women can. It's not a unique experience to mistake a toad for a prince. Tell me about your new man. He's an artist, you say. Italian?'

'No, no . . . English. He's David Warren.'

Jane looked startled. For once in her life she had no quick comment to make.

'I was renting his house at Portofino while he was away on a trip,' Liz explained. 'He came home unexpectedly. It would have been difficult for me to find somewhere else to live, so he suggested I stay on. It's a big roomy house. I was already in love with the Villa Delphini. Pretty soon I felt the same way about its owner.'

'I know you always liked his work,' said her agent. 'So do I. What's he like as a man? I don't believe I've ever seen a photograph of him. He's not a publicity-seeker. He doesn't need to be.'

'He's very tall . . . fair-haired . . . blue-eyed.' Liz resisted the temptation to extol David's charms at some length. If Jane hadn't guessed that she was in love with someone, she wouldn't have mentioned him.

She said, 'I was expecting you to be mad with curiosity about *Casimir's Cruise*. Since I told you about it on the telephone, have you gone off the idea?'

Jane said, 'Definitely not. I'm most eager to see it. Show me.'

They were sitting in a corner of the lounge before going through to the restaurant. From the leather briefcase containing half a dozen of her tiny canvasses, Liz produced the display book of clear plastic pockets which protected the paintings and the pages of text which made up her book.

'While you're looking through it, I'll go and freshen up. I had rather a rush to get here on time,' she said, rising to go to the powder room.

When she returned, Jane's dark hair which, regardless of changing fashions, she always wore in a long bob, was still hanging in two glossy curtains on either side of her thin face as she bent her head over the book.

She glanced up as Liz rejoined her, her grey eyes alight with enthusiasm.

'This is great, Liz, really terrific! Only the other day I was shown the winning entries for this year's Mother Goose Award. That's a prize—a bronze egg and a cheque—which is given annually to the most promising newcomer to British children's book illustration. I believe you could win it next year. This brush and pen work is first class and you've always had a superb colour sense. You must have spent hours cat-watching. Did you have time for any of your regular pictures?'

'Yes, I've brought six to show you,' said Liz, sitting down and producing them. 'The house at Portofino is a treasure trove of the kind of things I love to paint,' she explained. 'The background in this one is a piece of Fortuny silk which was being used to curtain a door at the back of a shoe-mender's shop. Goodness knows how it came there, but David recognised it and rescued it.'

She went on to tell Jane the history of some of the other objects she had included in the pictures.

Presently they moved to the Picnic Basket for lunch. When a waitress had taken their order for cottage cheese salads and a carafe of white wine, Jane said, 'It sounds to me as if you and David Warren were made for each other.'

'I hope so.'

Her agent gave her a shrewd glance. 'What's the problem? A wife in the background?'

'No, David has never been married, and I'm not

sure he ever will be. He's in his early forties. I don't
think he wants to have children. Why does he need to
marry?' She didn't confide her suspicion that he had
given his heart to a woman who would never belong to
him.

Jane said, 'In that case, my dear, you should give
some thought to the future. No woman who isn't
married should put herself in the position of having
nowhere to go when a love affair comes to an end. It
so happens that one of my other clients is about to go
off to Greece to share a place there with his boy-
friend. I think he's crazy—as I did when you were
persuaded to move in with Richard—but Lambert is
determined to give up his place here and I can't talk
him out of it. It's one huge room, stunningly
decorated. You know how clever gays are at that sort
of thing—better then we are, usually. Before it gets on
the grapevine that his place is up for grabs, why don't
you take a look? You should have a base somewhere,
Liz. Everyone needs their own bolt-hole.'

At first Liz resisted the suggestion on the grounds
that she was only in London until the following day
and had arranged to meet David for tea at Fortnum's.
Apart from other considerations, she hadn't time to
see the flat.

Jane dismissed these objections with a wave of the
hand. 'I know Lambert's place is perfect for you. It's a
chance in a thousand, and you shouldn't miss it. Then
whatever happens in the future, you won't be out on a
limb—as you were when you split up with Richard.'

Eventually, after much argument, she pressured the
younger woman into agreeing to let her telephone
Lambert and, if he were at home, to arrange an
immediate viewing in place of the shopping Liz had
planned for the interval between lunch with her agent
and tea with David.

It was after six when Liz walked back to the Cavendish, having agreed to sub-lease the flat for a year with an option to take over the whole of the remaining six-year lease at the end of that time.

The man she was leasing it from—an amusing personality with whom she could have talked shop for hours—had wanted to dispose of his lease on the place altogether. While not revealing her present connection, Liz had been frank about the mistake she had made giving up her previous flat in circumstances similar to his present intentions.

'I'm not completely sure I need a pied-à-terre in London. If I sub-lease from you for twelve months, we shall both have time to be certain we're doing the right thing,' she had pointed out. 'Your Greek island may be lovely for holidays, but perhaps not so good for year-round living.'

And you may go off your friend when you've shared a place with him for a while, was her unspoken afterthought.

Hurrying back to the hotel to change for the theatre, she was in two minds whether to tell David what she had done. Earlier she had left messages at the hotel and at their rendezvous so that he shouldn't be worried when she didn't turn up for tea.

If she didn't tell him about the flat, she would have to deceive him about her failure to appear at Fortnum's. Deception—especially with someone she loved—went against the grain with her.

On the other hand, how would he react if she did tell him?

If he had no thought of separation, the last thing she wanted to do was to introduce an idea which was not in his mind. At the same time she had to admit that having her own roof somewhere did make her feel more comfortable about her position as his girl-friend.

It also meant that, when they came to London again, instead of using a hotel they could stay at her place.

When she reached their room, David, already dressed to go to the theatre, was watching TV.

By nature alert to the small signs betraying people's feelings, she knew instantly he was annoyed. The way he sprang up from the chair, the way he snapped off the set and, most of all, his failure to smile as she walked in, warned her something had changed the mood he had been in when they parted before lunch.

'Next time you change your plans, it would be a good idea to leave a message for the person you were supposed to meet at the meeting place, not somewhere else,' he said curtly. 'I didn't get the message you left here until I'd spent an hour at Fortnum's, wondering if you'd jay-walked yourself under a taxi.'

'But I left two messages, one here and one at Fortnum's. I telephoned them right after my lunch with Jane. They assured me they'd let you know I couldn't make it.'

'Well, they didn't,' he said, with a snap.

'Did you ask if there was a message for you?'

'Naturally. When you hadn't turned up by twenty past four, I asked at the cash desk. No message. Eventually I came back here.'

'Oh, lord, I'm so sorry, David. But it really wasn't my fault. Whoever took the message must have gone off duty before you arrived and forgotten to leave the message with someone else. How maddening!'

Her explanation and apology didn't appear to calm his annoyance. His tone was still clipped, his face stern, as he said, 'Where have you been?'

The peremptory question took her back to the days when Barney had expected her to account for every hour of the time she didn't spend with him.

David's watchful expression, reminding her of the

groundless suspicions she had had to put up with from
Barney, made her own tone short as she answered,
'I've just walked all the way back from Chelsea
because I couldn't get a taxi. If you don't mind I'd
like a drink before you start shooting questions at me.
I also need to start changing if we're going to eat before
the theatre.'

For some seconds she had the feeling he wanted to
grab her and shake her. His eyes were like blue laser
beams, his mouth a hard angry line. This was a side of
his nature she had glimpsed before when he had been
annoyed with Toni, the Italian builder. But now he
was furious with her, his whole demeanour so
threatening that, when he moved towards her,
instinctively she stepped backwards.

It turned out he was making for the refrigerator.
'What would you like? Gin and tonic? Vodka?' he
asked, as he opened it.

'Gin and tonic, please.'

With fingers which were shaking slightly, Liz began
to unbutton her dress. She would have liked to take a
shower, but there wasn't time. She regretted now
staying so long, chatting to Lambert. As soon as she
had seen the flat and they had discussed the
instructions they would give their solicitors, she
should have come away, not stayed to drink sherry and
look at his Greek island sketchbook.

'What did you think I was going to do? Beat you
up?' David enquired sardonically, as he handed her
the drink.

'Of course not,' she answered quickly, adding, when
he arched a sceptical eyebrow, 'Shake me perhaps, as
you seem in rather a rage.'

'However much of a rage I'm in, I don't manhandle
women,' he said coldly. His eyes narrowed intently.
'Did your last lover? Is that why you left him?'

'Certainly not! Richard wasn't that sort of brute. If he had been, I shouldn't have spent three weeks with him, let alone three years.'

'Some women do stay with men who knock them about.'

'Only if they have no option . . . nowhere else to go,' said Liz. 'I never heard of a woman who could manage on her own staying with a brutal man.'

He was refilling the glass which he had been holding, empty, when she entered the room.

'I've heard of stranger things than that. Some women will take all kinds of punishment—mental and physical—if they're in love or infatuated. They don't seem able to help themselves.'

His voice had an odd, brooding note which made her wonder if, as he spoke, he was thinking of someone he knew. Was it possible his sister-in-law had endured some form of cruelty at the hands of her husband and David had known of it and hated his brother, even wanted to kill him?

She had been about to retort that in that case the women must be masochists because in the Western world there was no reason for anyone to endure serious ill-treatment, but she changed her mind. The thought of what David must have suffered if, for some unfathomable reason, the woman he loved had chosen to stay married to a man who abused her, caused a surge of love to sweep through her.

'David, you kissed me goodbye. Aren't you going to kiss me hello?' she said, in a gentler voice, going to where he was standing and smiling at him, her eyes soft.

But her move to make peace between them did not meet with the quick contrition for his crossness which she expected.

His face remained guarded, unfriendly. 'How long will it take you to change?'

'Not long ... not more than ten minutes. Oh, darling, don't stay in a huff.' The endearment slipped out before she could stop it.

At that his lean features did relax slightly, but he chose to ignore the suggestion that he kiss her.

'How did your lunch go? What did Jane think of the book?'

'She's enthusiastic ... and she liked all the paintings, especially the one with the Fortuny silk as a background. After lunch she wanted me to meet Lambert Radley. He's also a client of hers and as he's leaving for Greece soon, to go and live there, today was my only chance to see him. He's a homosexual,' she added, 'so one can visit his flat without any danger of being pounced on.'

It was the truth, but not the whole truth. That would keep for a more propitious moment when David's mood was less combustible. Instinct told her now wasn't the time to announce the real reason she had been to see Lambert.

By the time she had finished accounting for her afternoon, David's deeply tanned face had resumed its normal expression of good humour.

He actually smiled as he said, 'So you stood me up for a gay. Flattering!'

Relieved that the flare-up was over, she said, 'You would like Lambert, David. Don't pull a face! He's not conspicuously gay and he has stunning taste. His flat is my idea of heaven ... next to your villa.'

Twenty-four hours later they were back on the terrace at the Villa Delphini, the visit to London a memory. Mostly a happy memory, except for that one short outbreak of conflict between them.

'I'm glad to be back, aren't you?' said David, leaning on the balustrade, watching a power boat

racing across the blue sea, the roar of its engine
reduced, at this height and distance, to the sonorous
drone of a bumble-bee. 'Two days in a city is long
enough.'

'Yes, I'm very glad to be back. I missed the pool
and the view and the peace of it here,' Liz agreed.
'Tomorrow I'm going to start work on Casimir's next
adventure.'

In the days that followed, as their life resumed its
quiet pattern of work, conversation, reading, dinners
at Luigi's and nights—sometimes afternoons—in each
other's arms, Liz had the feel that here at Portofino
they were safe. In other places they were not.
Something bad might happen, as it had in London
when they had almost quarrelled.

In spite of her rapid recovery from the operation,
Anna's convalescence at Pisa had received a setback.
One of the grandchildren had brought chickenpox into
the household, and Anna, having somehow escaped
the illness in her own childhood and when her
children had it, had thereupon had it very badly.
When she was in a fit state for David and Liz to visit
her, she was still looking poorly. Her daughter was
hoping to persuade her to remain at Pisa permanently.

'She is too old to work, Signor. For the rest of her
life she should rest,' the daughter told David.

'Not my idea of rest; being surrounded by children,
with a television blaring all day and neighbours
popping in and out,' he said to Liz, as they drove
home.

'Still it's nice that they want her to be there.'

She thought of herself at Anna's age and wondered
where she would be living. But old age was so far, far
ahead that she couldn't imagine it. The future could
take care of itself. Even next year was a time she
preferred to ignore. Today, this afternoon, this hour

was all she wanted to think about. Being with David, being happy . . . now.

Sometimes, however, the post brought reminders that there was another less peaceful world outside their sunlit haven. Jane wrote that a leading British publisher of children's books was interested in Casimir, and an American tie-in was being negotiated. Liz showed those letters to David and discussed them with him.

When she received a letter from her solicitor, enclosing papers to be signed, she realised she still hadn't mentioned leasing Lambert's flat.

David was far too well-bred to show any interest in her post unless she brought it to his attention. Nevertheless she felt guilty at keeping something important from him. She felt all right about not showing him a statement from her bank or corre-spondence relating to her modest investments. But the matter of the flat pricked her conscience; yet somehow she couldn't bring herself to talk to him about it.

After worrying about it for some days, she decided to keep it as a surprise for the next time they went to London. Then, before he rang up the Cavendish, she would say it wouldn't be necessary to stay at a hotel because she had the use of a flat, mainly to store her belongings, but also as a pied-à-terre.

The day it all came to an end began like any other day.

Because of his nocturnal habits, David had an alarm on his watch which he used to make sure he always woke up early. Having stopped the insistent buzz, which had half-wakened Liz, he would kiss her fully awake and they would lie in each other's arms for a few minutes. Sometimes, if they hadn't made love the night before, this would delay their early rising.

Either way, sooner or later, he would go to his

bathroom and she to hers. Later they would meet in the kitchen to share the breakfast preparations.

The sun would be warming the eastern end of the terrace by the time the tray was ready. David would carry the tray outside and she would bring the squabs and cushions from the basket chairs which were brought indoors overnight to prevent dew from making them damp.

After breakfast they would separate to work from nine until noon.

Sometimes David would work through till evening without a break. But mostly, now that his travel sketches were in order, he emerged from his studio soon after twelve to join her in a swim before lunch. By that time the post had arrived and the various travel and art magazines to which he had airmail subscriptions, although he had allowed these to lapse during his absence.

On the day when this peaceful routine took place for the last time, Liz had spent the morning painting a single daisy stuck in a Chinese snuff bottle of carved pink quartz.

In the evening they were going to a party at one of the neighbouring villas which was the holiday house of a wealthy family from Milan. It would be an opportunity for her to wear an outfit she had bought in London but which David hadn't seen yet.

It would be the first party they had ever been to together and she was looking forward to it. Although the Salviatis were very rich manufacturers and their villa was furnished in an ultra-modern style, their fortune had been founded two generations earlier and they had a discriminating eye for the best in modern design, David had told her. He felt sure she would like them.

He always finished his swim several minutes before

she did. They both swam twenty lengths of the pool, a distance of about a quarter of a mile, but he was by far the more powerful swimmer. When she wasn't in the pool with him, she loved to watch the apparently effortless rhythm of his arms scything through the water.

On the morning of the party he had already gone up to the upper terrace by the time she finished her last lap and swung up the metal ladder at the deep end. She swam naked first thing in the morning. They both did. After she had dried, she put on a dry bikini and a loose white T-shirt. Then she let down her plait which had been pinned to the top of her head so that most of her hair was still dry.

When Liz reached the upper terrace, Teresa, who came every day now, had finished arranging their light lunch on the table under the sunbrella. David was reading a letter.

The fact that he didn't get up to pull out her chair for her should have been an early warning that something was wrong. Normally he was a man who never neglected the small everyday courtesies which made a woman feel cherished. However, at present he was totally immersed in what he was reading and, judging by his frown, the news contained in the letter wasn't good.

Before sitting down, Liz lifted the lemon which served as a stopper in the mouth of the dark green glass carafe of white wine.

The use of lemons as stoppers was an idea David had borrowed from Madame Romain Gary, better known as Lesley Blanch, the traveller and writer whose books with their romantic titles, *Pavilions of the Heart* and *Sabres of Paradise*, had long been among Liz's favourites.

To discover that David had actually been invited to

a small, exclusive buffet supper at Madame Gary's house in France, close to the Italian border, had filled her with envy. From the way he described it, the writer's house, crammed with the memorabilia of a lifetime's wanderings, was very much like his own beautiful house. Everything he had told her about Lesley Blanch—from the food she had given her guests to the way she dressed—had intensified her admiration for one of the world's most interesting women.

She had filled his glass and her own, and was sitting down, spreading a napkin across her bare legs, when David folded the letter and replaced it in its envelope. Although he reached for the glass of wine she had poured for him, she could see his mind was miles away.

'Is anything the matter, David?' she asked, with the first premonition of impending disaster.

He looked at her then, and what she saw in his eyes filled her with dread. Before he spoke, she knew their golden world was about to disintegrate; that after today it would never be the same again.

'I shall have to go to England first thing tomorrow,' he told her. 'Something has happened—something most unexpected—which I think is going to change my life.'

'You mean ... at Blackmead?' she asked, in a low strained voice.

'Yes, at Blackmead. How did you guess?'

CHAPTER FIVE

A WASP flew in from the brightness surrounding their circle of shade. It hovered over the salad, deciding where to alight. David waved it away.

Liz didn't answer his question. In spite of the burning heat, she felt suddenly cold.

'What's happened?' she asked him.

'Margaret—my sister-in-law—has received a proposal of marriage which she's decided to accept. It means she'll be leaving Blackmead. The estate is entailed. It's always been mine officially, but I couldn't live there as long as she was in residence. Now, if I want to, I can go back and take over. At one time I didn't want to, but now ... perhaps I do. I'll have to think it over.'

She stared at him, baffled. He didn't sound as if Margaret Castle's impending marriage had come as a shattering blow to him. Could it be that he didn't care for her any more? That at last he was cured of his love for her?

'Who is she going to marry?' she asked, watching him closely.

'One of my brother's hunting cronies whose wife died a few months ago. His house is much larger and more important than Blackmead. She'll be making a change for the better,' David said drily. 'Bob is a crashing bore, but that won't worry Margaret as long as she's improving her position socially and financially.'

The open contempt in his tone made her realise she must have been wildly wide of the mark in thinking him in love with Margaret. But if she hadn't been the important woman in his life, who had? There must have been *someone*.

'There was a time when Bob wouldn't have remarried until his wife had been in the vault at least a year,' he went on matter-of-factly. 'But it seems the old order changeth, even with his generation. He's a randy old brute, so I've heard. Reading between the lines, Margaret is already warming his bed and wants to make it official as soon as possible. Hence the urgent summons.' He picked up the large fork and spoon for use with the salad and offered them to her.

Liz had been hungry when she came up from the pool. Now her appetite had deserted her. The feeling of suffocating panic she had felt when he said something had happened which would change his life—and hers—had passed. But a sense of unease still lingered.

She forced herself to act calmly, as if nothing crucial had happened. 'How long do you expect to be over there? I suppose you have no idea,' she said, as she took a small helping of Teresa's egg salad.

'Not really, at this stage—no. You'll come with me, won't you? I hope so.'

He looked and sounded sincere. Her heart leapt with joy.

She forced herself to say coolly, 'Oh, but won't you be better on your own? I'm an outsider. I should be an encumbrance.'

David handed the pepper grinder to her. 'I realise it's rather a drag leaving here while the weather's still lovely, which it may not be in England. But when it's a warm September, it's very fine countryside round there. There's no pool, but there are some good walks. I don't think you'd find it too deadly. If we weren't together all day, we should still be together all night. Which is pretty important to me, and I hope to you, too.'

She kept her gaze on her plate so that he shouldn't guess *how* important it was to her.

'Bob isn't the only one who needs his bed warming, hm?' she said lightly. 'Very well, I'll come. Is Blackmead anywhere near Coventry? I've always wanted to see Graham Sutherland's Crucifixion tapestry in the cathedral.'

'Coventry isn't far. The main place of interest near us is Althorp, Earl Spencer's place. It wasn't a mecca for tourists when I was a boy. But that was before his daughter became England's darling.'

'Have you met the Princess of Wales?'

He shook his head. 'Margaret has, I believe. But she'd be impressed whether the girl was a charmer or not.'

'I'm sure she is a charmer,' said Liz. 'She's certainly charming to look at.'

David drank some wine. 'While I was in Australia, the *Sydney Morning Herald* ran an Australia Day piece by a writer called Patrick White in which he referred to Diana as the Prince's "clotheshorse waxwork of a wife". It was an article which contained a good deal of sense about Australian patriotism, but he ruined it by the offensive remark about Diana. A week later the paper printed a lot of indignant letters from Aussies who wanted to dissociate themselves from his boorishness.'

'Are you a royalist?' she asked.

There was still so much she had to learn about him; so many corners of his mind still hidden from her. It baffled her that after a few years of marriage some people had nothing to say to each other. She felt she could listen to David talking for ever. And never run out of things she wanted to tell him.

But he might not feel the same way.

*   *   *

They were welcomed to the Salviatis' party by Giancarlo, the good-looking son of the house. Learning that Liz was also an artist, he asked if she would like to see his father's collection of paintings by Giorgio Morandi, the Italian master of still life.

She had happened to see a retrospective exhibition of Morandi's work at the Guggenheim Museum in New York and had been fascinated by it, and by the artist himself.

Morandi had never married. Until his death in 1964, he had lived in Bologna, where he was a professor of engraving, with his three spinster sisters. Money hadn't been important to him. Even when he was famous, he had charged almost nothing for his pictures. People who asked him for one had been put on a list. He had painted little else but bottles which he bought in flea markets. His studio had been famous for its dustiness; the dust which lay over everything softening the light and colour.

Giancarlo's father had paintings dating back to 1925 when Morandi had begun to concentrate on studies of jugs, bottles and vases. They were all together in one room and his son stayed with her, chatting, while she looked at them. He seemed in no hurry to resume his duties as one of the hosts. She suspected he might have been deputed by his parents to find out about her.

By the time they returned to the main *salone*, many other people had arrived. The party was in full swing with champagne flowing and hired waiters circulating with platters of delicious mouthfuls.

From time to time, in the next hour, Liz saw David talking and laughing with groups of people he knew. Once or twice their eyes met. Seeing her surrounded by attentive Italians, he grinned and flickered a wink.

It was while she was talking to an Italian woman about her passion for Missoni knits that another woman overheard her and joined in their conversation.

In the way of parties, a few minutes later Liz and the newcomer were on their own, whereupon she introduced herself. 'I'm Natasha Lunardi. My parents were Russian, I was born in London and I'm married to a Italian.'

Liz had noticed her earlier because she was stunningly well dressed.

She said, 'How do you do? I'm Liz Redwood. Half American, half British.'

'You're David's new girl-friend, aren't you?' Natasha said pleasantly.

How do *you* know that? Liz wondered.

She said, 'Yes, I am.'

'Welcome to the club. So was I, a few years ago. But please don't tell my husband. Andrea's insanely jealous. He wouldn't like it if he knew I'd been even briefly involved with a man with David's reputation. And it was exceedingly brief. You've no need to be jealous. At least not of *me*,' Natasha added.

Liz stared at her, momentarily tongue-tied. She had never had to cope with a situation like this before. Part of her wanted to tell Natasha to get lost; and part of her wanted to know what she meant by 'David's reputation' and that cryptic 'not of *me*'.

Natasha didn't wait to be prompted. She said, 'You look a nice girl. I'd hate to see you get hurt as badly as I was, so I'll stick my neck out and tell you a couple of things which everyone else will keep quiet about. David is an incorrigible stud who makes it with every woman who comes his way. He's trying to forget an affair he had here a few years ago. It was kinky to say the least. The girl was about seventeen and she was his niece. She was sent here to learn Italian and he seduced her. She had an unusual name. Bethany . . . Bethany Castle. Ask him about her.'

At this point a middle-aged man, recognisably Giancarlo's father, came up and said warmly, in perfect English, 'Miss Redwood, I'm Carlo Salviati. What a pleasure to meet you! My son tells me you are also an admirer of Morandi. May I show you some other paintings which I think may interest you? You will excuse us, Signora Lunardi. I know your interest is sculpture.'

He whisked Liz away to look at some abstract paintings. Later he introduced her to his wife whose dark eyes swiftly assessed her clothes and her cameo ornaments.

Hard as it was for Liz to concentrate on anything but the bombshell Natasha had tossed at her, she did her best to listen to Signora Salviati's explanation of why Milan had replaced Rome as the design capital of Italy.

'Valentino still shows his collections in Roma, but that is high fashion for the very rich woman. The designers for ready-to-wear are those with the greatest influence and they are all in Milano . . . Giorgio Armani, Gianfranco Ferre, Gianni Versace and many others. That is because fashion begins with fabrics. Milano is near the factories at Lake Como where most of our beautiful Italian fabrics are manufactured,' she explained.

'Is that your husband's business, Signora?' Liz asked.

Her hostess nodded. 'Perhaps you have never heard of such firms as Bini, Mantero, Ratti, Taroni and Salviati, but to connoisseurs of fabrics they are names as famous as da Vinci and Canaletto in the world of art. What you are wearing? Is it by an English designer?'

Liz glanced down at her clothes; linen pants, a brief linen chemise, both black, teamed with a gauzy coat of black and white linen voile.

'Yes, this is by Caroline Charles, who is one of Britain's best ready-to-wear designers.'

The older woman put out a manicured hand to touch one diaphanous sleeve caught into a cuff with two small self-covered buttons. 'But perhaps she finds her fabrics in Italy.'

They continued talking about fashion until Giancarlo appeared beside them.

'Mama, I have done my duty and spoken to all the old ladies. Now I want to enjoy myself by taking this pretty young lady round the garden. I have asked David's permission.'

His mother said, 'I hope you and David will have dinner with us soon, Miss Redwood. I look forward to having another talk with you.'

'And I with you, Signora . . . but please call me Liz.'

Her hostess acknowledged this with a smiling nod before she moved away.

'Have I also permission to use your first name?' her son enquired, taking Liz's arm and steering her out of one of the three double doors which gave on to a terrace more opulently furnished than David's.

'Of course. I mean to use yours,' she answered, forcing a smile. 'Are you always so formal, Giancarlo? Permission to show me the garden. Permission to use my first name!'

'Sometimes I am formal . . . sometimes very informal.' He paused to replace her empty champagne glass on the tray of a hovering waiter, and to take two full glasses. 'Unfortunately I have an unfounded reputation for being what you call a ladies' man. Therefore I'm particularly careful to behave correctly with beautiful girls who belong to other men.'

There was a time when her first reaction would have been to refute the suggestion that she belonged to anyone. Now to belong to David, and to have him belong to her, was a state she longed for. She was tempted to say, 'I thought it was David who had that reputation,' but thought better of it.

What she did say was, 'Then I advise you never to ask permission to take Signora Lunardi round the garden. She tells me her husband is a ferociously jealous man.'

'Understandably. Not only is he thirty years older than Natasha, but he must know she married him for his money, the stupid old goat,' the young Italian replied, with surprising bluntness. 'I saw her talking to you. I don't think she is a woman with whom you could be friends. To tell you the truth, she wouldn't be invited to this house except that old Lunardi is a friend of the family and we can't exclude him from our parties because he has married a gold-digging bitch.'

'A bitch?' Liz echoed, raising her eyebrows. 'I thought she was once a friend of David's? She claims to be.'

He shook his head. 'She would have liked that, but she wasn't. She never lived under his roof. I was present the day she realised she wasn't getting anywhere with him and showed herself in her true colours. What a scene she made! Then she went back to the hotel, which is where she got her claws into Lunardi.'

Like the terrace, the grounds surrounding his parents' house were more elaborate than the gardens of the Villa Delphini. Liz preferred the old-fashioned scented roses, cascades of bougainvillaea and over-flowing urns of geraniums in David's garden to the orderly beds of modern hybrid roses and neatly clipped cypress hedges of this garden.

As they strolled round the large Roman pool, she said, 'You must have known David's niece, Bethany.'

'Yes, very well. I used to take her out sometimes. She was very young . . . seventeen. She had never been out with a man before me. David warned me he would break my neck if I didn't behave myself properly,' he said, with a reminiscent grin. 'She was a sweet girl, Bethany. When you meet her, you will agree.'

'Where does she live now?'

'In a famous castle in the southern part of England. Her father-in-law is the Duke of Dorset. Bethany and her husband have an apartment in the castle. I've been invited to stay with them, but I haven't been yet. In winter I like to spend my holidays skiing, and in summer to go to Cavallo.'

This, he explained to her, was a Mediterranean island between Corsica and Sardinia where he had a studio-apartment in the style of a Corsican shepherd's hut, and where he spent his time scuba-diving round the many ships wrecked round the island.

While he was telling her about the place, David joined them.

'I'm going to take Liz home now, Giancarlo. We're travelling to England tomorrow and we haven't finished our packing.'

Walking back to the Villa Delphini a short time later, he said, 'Drinks parties aren't my favourite form of entertainment. God knows what the bill for tonight's little beanfeast will be. Whatever it is, the Salviatis can well afford it. But for my money I'd sooner share a basket of figs and a bottle of Chianti with you than stand around swilling champagne and eating bits of pastry with most of that crowd.'

Liz murmured agreement. At this moment she didn't even want to be with him. She longed for some time alone to mull over what Natasha had told her and what Giancarlo had said about Natasha.

When David had unlocked the door, she said, 'I'm going up to change. I shan't be long.'

'I'll heat the soup and lay a tray,' he answered. Accompanied by crusty bread, Teresa's vegetable soups were a meal in themselves.

At the top of the staircase she didn't turn towards their room. Obeying an impulse, she walked the length of the landing to the room where Bethany had slept during her stay at the Villa.

Liz hadn't believed for a second Natasha's accusation that David had seduced his niece. A womaniser he might be; but not the kind of man who would take advantage of any sheltered seventeen-year-old, let alone his brother's child.

But it wasn't impossible that he loved her. Even brothers and sisters who hadn't been brought up together had been known to fall in love. First cousins often did. A blood relationship didn't inoculate people against loving each other, and if the girl was as charming as Giancarlo made out . . .

She sighed, quietly closing the door. The divorce rate proved the perishability of married love. How strange that when it was thwarted, love seemed to grow stronger, not weaker.

The motorail train which ran from Milan to Boulogne twice a week in the holiday season left the Porta Garibaldi at nine in the evening.

The Ferrari was loaded earlier, leaving them time to have dinner in a restaurant recommended by Giancarlo before finding the first class sleeper reserved for them and unpacking their light hand luggage.

The compartment had two bunks, one above the other, and a washbasin. It was the first time since they had begun sleeping together that they had spent a night in separate beds. David kissed her good night before disappearing beneath her. He had suggested Liz should occupy the upper bunk because it had unrestricted headroom. He knew she disliked confined spaces.

They had shared another bottle of wine while the train began its long journey across Europe, and this made her sleepy. His reading light was still on when she lay down and closed her eyes, finding the noise and motion of the train soporific rather than disturbing.

During the night she woke up, thirsty. Fortunately David had had the forethought to bring water on board as well as wine. She was able to quench her thirst, but not to get back to sleep.

For a long time she lay awake, wondering if they would ever return to Portofino together, or if it had been a period of her life which had come to an end, *finito*, but which she would remember until she died.

It had been like a long, wonderful honeymoon, and perhaps it wasn't over yet. But surely, if David had the capacity to love her, he would have begun by now?

She knew how easily women in love could delude themselves that a man was beginning to care for them. She had spent hours of her life listening to girl friends telling the things *he* had said and done to convince them he was becoming seriously involved. Often Liz had doubted that *he* had anything more in mind than what he was already getting.

However, it was easy to be detached about other people's love lives; much harder to apply clear-eyed judgment to one's own.

When David had said . . . *we should still be together all night. Which is pretty important to me, and I hope to you, too*, she had felt a wild leap of the heart.

But much as she wanted to interpret that statement to mean that her presence was becoming increasingly necessary to him, she knew it might mean nothing more than that he found their liaison enjoyable and convenient at the moment, but perhaps not forever.

She remembered reading a book about man–woman relationships in which the author had written—'cliff-hanging sex only lasts about three years or less with people in close proximity'.

Maybe David didn't see any reason to let his sex life dull down. But she didn't really believe Natasha Lunardi's allegation that he was an incorrigible stud, forever seeking fresh conquests. Men like that were easily recognisable. David was a mature stable personality. What was holding him back from making a long-term commitment wasn't the inability to love only one woman, but rather the inability to forget the girl called Bethany.

They had brought fruit with them to supplement the breakfast served on the train as it crossed France, and books to read when looking at the scenery palled.

They arrived at Boulogne at noon and the car was unloaded in time for them to catch a Hovercraft which reached Dover soon after two. Having nothing to declare, they were soon through Customs and on the road to London.

'David, are you sure it might not be better if you dropped me off in London and spent the first couple of nights at Blackmead on your own?' Liz said, as they reached the outskirts.

'Not better for me. Is that an oblique way of saying you want to be dropped off? Are you itching to talk to Jane?'

'No, I can do that by telephone. I suppose the truth is I'm nervous of meeting your sister-in-law. You've made her sound rather daunting. I don't think we'll be *en rapport*.'

'I'm certain you won't,' he said drily. 'She's a dreadful female. But she won't be unpleasant to you.'

'I'm sure she will disapprove of me ... of our relationship.'

'Let her. I don't give a damn for Margaret's opinion. She almost broke Bethany's heart by having Mossy, her cat, destroyed while she was away at school. She was an appallingly unkind stepmother, probably because she was jealous of my brother's first wife whom Bethany strongly resembled,' he said, in a grim tone.

Once through London, they were more than halfway to their destination. As the Ferrari swept along the MI, her wakeful night caught up with her. She dozed.

When she opened her eyes, they were leaving the motorway by the slip road to Northampton. This part of England was new to her. She looked at the countryside with interest, although, the weather having turned to rain, the woods looked sodden, the fields bleak under a sullen grey sky.

'Not far now,' said David, taking his eyes off the wet road long enough to smile at her. 'You must be longing for a drink and a bath. I can't promise you a good dinner, I'm afraid. The last time I was at home the cook was good at making cakes, but not so hot with meat and vegetables.'

He called it home, she noticed, with dismay. Had he already decided to give up the house in Italy and return to this uncertain climate? Perhaps because she was tired, Northamptonshire didn't strike her as a county where *she* wanted to live, although anywhere with David would be better than living without him.

*   *   *

An hour later, lying in a hot bath with a gin and tonic perched on the ledge of polished mahogany surrounding the tub, her spirits lifted a little.

David was in the bedroom, unpacking his case. As dinner at Blackmead Manor was at seven-fifteen there hadn't been time for a long chat with Lady Castle. She had greeted them both quite pleasantly, but Liz had sensed that she had as little time for her brother-in-law as he for her.

He came to stand in the doorway. 'Don't pull out the plug when you've finished. I'll bath in your water. Want me to scrub your back?'

'Yes, please, that would be lovely.'

She sat up and sipped her drink while he took off his clothes before taking her face-cloth and applying soap to it. Then he knelt by the side of the bath and began to lather her back.

'Mm ... luxury,' she murmured presently, as he rinsed away the lather with handfuls of water.

Then she gasped as his other hand slipped under her arm to stroke her wet breasts.

'Move forward. I'm coming in with you.'

Causing a tidal wave which swept dangerously close to the rim, he climbed in behind her and drew her into his arms, one hand returning to her breasts, the other gliding under the surface of the water.

The Victorian bath with its brass taps, one marked *Rain*, was sufficiently deep and wide to accommodate them both in comfort. It had a slope for David to lean on and she lay against his chest, his long legs spread on either side of her hips.

'I missed you last night,' he said softly, close to her ear.

Later, they dressed in a hurry and went down to eat a meal which was even worse than David had prophesied.

It began with clear vegetable soup, recognisably made from a packet, served by an elderly woman who was introduced as Miss Evans, but called Nanny by Lady Castle, who had changed into an ankle-length kilt and a black turtle-neck top with a diamond horse brooch pinned to her large jutting bosom.

Next came a leg of lamb brought in by another woman who was Mrs Herring, the cook. She had a good look at Liz before returning to the kitchen.

Margaret Castle stood up to carve, Nanny beside her, waiting to take the plates round. Liz was dismayed to see three large slices of meat, each with a crescent of fat, arranged on the first plate.

To her relief, David said, 'I'll have that one, Nanny. Only one thin slice for Liz, please, Margaret. She has a very small appetite.'

His sister-in-law shot a glance at her guest's slender figure which was not approving.

The sprouts had been boiled to death. The peas had been frozen. The mashed potatoes had either been cooked too long or were reconstituted.

Eating Mrs Herring's calamities as heartily as if they had come from Albert Roux's kitchen, Lady Castle talked about her daughters, Susan and Julia, who were still at school. She seemed amazed to discover Liz had been educated at the same establishment; and even more astonished when David remarked that the school had been Liz's grandfather's house.

'My eldest daughter, Bethany, is married,' she continued. Turning to David, she asked, 'Did you know the Dorsets' elder son died of that frightful illness soon after Bethany's wedding?'

'Yes, she wrote to me.' He looked across the table at Liz. 'Bethany's brother-in-law had a rare wasting disease for which there's no effective treatment yet.

His death in his early thirties was a terrible blow to his parents. Bethany's marriage to Robert, their younger son, and the fact that she had a son within a year of the wedding helped them to cope with James' death.'

He spoke in an oddly flat tone. She wondered what Bethany's marriage had done to him. If she had to live through David's marriage to someone else, the pain would be almost unbearable.

If she had had any doubts that he still cared for Bethany, they would have been quashed by what he had said in the car that afternoon. Only when men loved women did they remember such details as the name of the loved one's childhood pet. Mossy. He wouldn't have remembered that if Mossy's owner hadn't been, and still was, the light of his life whose youthful distress could, years later, make him angry.

The pudding was stewed plums with blancmange. Liz thought this must be one of the last country houses in England where an uninspired cook was still tolerated.

'These are our own plums,' Lady Castle announced. 'The kitchen garden isn't what it was. Jackson is getting past it. You'll have to replace him, David. If you can. In spite of all the unemployment we hear about, it's impossible to get any reliable help in the house or garden.'

'What do you pay him?' he asked.

When she told him, David said drily, 'I'm surprised you've kept him so long. Very few people will work for less than the State will pay them when they're out of work. Why should they indeed? Would you?'

Her high colour deepened. '*I* should never live on the dole when I could be gainfully employed. That's what's wrong with the world today——'

He stemmed the incipient tirade by continuing quietly, 'I expect I shall replace Jackson if I advertise the job at a reasonable wage. There are a lot of young people who are turning back to the land and the old skills and crafts. But not for the wage you're paying him.'

His sister-in-law bristled. 'I don't think you realise what it costs to keep up a house of this size, my dear David,' she began irritably.

Liz waited until her hostess was obliged to draw breath. Then she seized the chance to say quickly, 'Would you think it rude if I left you to discuss these family matters and went to bed early, Lady Castle? I had a rather broken night on the train and I feel very tired.'

'By all means. Do go up, Miss Redwood,' the older woman said curtly.

David saw Liz to the door. 'I shan't be late,' he murmured, giving her a wink.

The bedroom had two radiators, but they were cold. She wondered when the central heating was turned on. Perhaps not until October, although on a wet night like this some form of warmth was needed, if only an electric fan heater.

When he telephoned Margaret from Italy, David must have made it clear he expected a double room, otherwise they would have been put in separate rooms. Liz felt sure that Nanny and the cook regarded her as a scarlet woman.

She hadn't expected the bed to have an electric blanket, but she was surprised not to find an old-fashioned hot water bottle warming the sheets. It was a long time since she'd had to get into a cold bed.

Thinking about the conversation before she left the dining-room, she wondered if David did know anything about the practical side of owning a large house in England; a house which needed considerable improvements to make it attractive and comfortable.

Basically the Manor was a fine eighteenth-century house which in more recent times had been lived in by several generations of people with no eye for beauty, no taste. The way Margaret Castle dressed and the food she allowed on her table were proof that she wasn't a stylish, domesticated woman.

Liz was domesticated. Apart from her flair for cooking, when she had had a place of her own she had enjoyed making it as attractive and welcoming as possible. By nature and training she found it easy to judge when rooms needed strong, warm colours to make them cosier, and when soft cool colours were needed.

She knew she could thoroughly enjoy putting Blackmead to rights—if she had the time and the incentive. But it would be an extremely time-consuming project which could only be done at the expense of her work.

Was she prepared to make that sacrifice for a man who was not her husband, and perhaps never would be?

Deeply troubled by all the shocks and changes of the past forty-eight hours, she put out the light and curled in a ball, trying to get warm.

When she woke the next morning the sun was shining and she was alone in the bed, only the imprint of a head on the other pillow showing that David had spent the night with her.

Looking out of the window, a few minutes later, she was surprised to see him riding up the drive and then disappearing from view where it forked, one way curving round to the front of the house and the other disappearing behind it, presumably to stables and coach-houses.

Ten minutes later, when she was almost dressed, he strode into the bedroom.

'I had no idea you could ride,' she said, after he had hugged and kissed her.

'No son of my father could have grown up without knowing how to sit a horse. It was never one of my favourite activities. Margaret is going to be out all day—some long-standing engagement she can't break. She left a few minutes ago. We'll be on our own until dinner, so I can show you round without her breathing down our necks. Are you ready to go down and count the lumps in Mrs Herring's porridge?'

After breakfast they explored the Manor from cellar to attic, from potting shed to butler's pantry. The only rooms they didn't enter were Lady Castle's bedroom and those of her daughters.

'This is where Bethany slept,' David told her, standing in one of the attics. 'Like Cinderella stuck up in a garret, poor kid.'

'It's not exactly comfy,' Liz agreed, looking round.

But, from what Giancarlo had told her, the 'sweet girl' who had once slept here had, like Cinderella, had a happy ending in store for her. She wondered if David was thinking the same thing, and wishing he could have been Bethany's Prince Charming.

A week later they went to London for a couple of nights so that Liz could meet the publishers who wanted to buy *Casimir's Cruise* and David could confer with his family solicitors.

On the second day they were in Jermyn Street together when a man turned away from a shop window and said, 'Hello, Warren. What brings you to England?'

If she had noticed him in passing, Liz would have taken him for a tall Italian. He had black hair and very dark eyes and his face seemed vaguely familiar.

He looked about ten years younger than David and was wearing a lightweight tweed suit and a rather boldly checked shirt, suggesting that his usual habitat was in the country.

'Robert ... how are you?' said David, shaking hands. He turned to her. 'This is Bethany's husband, Lord Hartigan ... Miss Liz Redwood.'

The dark man shook hands with her, his clasp less forceful than the bone-crushing grip the two men had exchanged.

'How do you do? You aren't by any chance Liz Redwood, the artist?'

As she never thought of herself as a well-known person, even in a modest way, the question surprised her. She nodded.

'You're one of my wife's favourite painters,' he told her. 'I've brought her several of your pictures for birthday and Christmas presents, and my mother has one. I'm on my way to meet Bethany for lunch. Are you free to join us? It would be a delightful surprise for her.'

David said, 'As a matter of fact I'd be very glad of a talk with you, Robert. You're the very man to give me some sound advice. We were going to have a snack in the Fountain, but we'd be delighted to join you. Where are you meeting Bethany?'

'Up the road ... only a few minutes' walk away,' said her husband.

Flanked by the two tall men with their markedly contrasting colouring—Lord Hartigan was less tanned, but had a naturally olive skin and evidently spent most of his time out of doors—Liz walked in the direction of St James's.

Her reactions to this unexpected opportunity to meet the girl who was so often in her thoughts were mixed. She wanted to meet her yet dreaded it. The alacrity with which David had accepted the invitation, without even an interrogative glance at her, gave her a sinking feeling that he was like an alcoholic who had been on the waggon a long time and was now on the point of taking the first fatal drink which would revive his addiction. Yet he must know how futile it was to go on secretly yearning for another man's wife.

When they came to the edge of the kerb on the east side of St James's, both men put a hand under her elbow to steer her across the busy thoroughfare.

A few minutes later they were mounting the steps of the Ritz Hotel, standing back for her to precede them through the revolving door into a quiet lobby with what seemed like a quarter of a mile of thick carpet leading along a wide lofty corridor. At the far end she glimpsed tall windows with the trees of Green Park beyond them.

'We're not due to meet for five minutes yet but, knowing Bethany, she'll be here before us. She's incurably early for every appointment, God bless her,' her husband remarked, after a member of the staff in dark livery with discreet touches of gold braid had said, 'Good morning, m'lord,' as they passed the porter's desk.

When they arrived at the Palm Court lounge, his wife was indeed there before them. She was seated on a striped brocade sofa in a mirrored alcove, her head bent over a book. Her hair was a rich reddish brown of Spanish mahogany and it was immediately obvious that she must be an extremely tall girl.

Engrossed in her book, she didn't see them approaching. It wasn't until Robert said, 'Hello, darling,' that she looked up, her eyes lighting at the sight of him.

Then she saw who was with him and the beautiful

large grey eyes widened and her mouth opened in a silent gasp.

Casting aside the book, she jumped to her feet, her lovely face glowing with pleasure.

'David! I can't believe it!' She flung her arms round him.

As he returned her embrace, David had his back to Liz, but she could see his face reflected in the panels of mirror at the back of the sofa. She had never seen an expression more clearly indicative of a man in seventh heaven—which, for him, was the ante-room to hell.

'And David isn't the only surprise I've brought you,' said Lord Hartigan, as his wife and her father's brother drew apart. 'Here is someone you've often said you wished you could meet. Miss Liz Redwood.'

Until he completed the introduction, it was clear that his wife found it difficult to drag her gaze away from David. But when he told her Liz's name, another look of astonished delight irradiated her features. Turning towards the older girl, she held out both hands to seize the one Liz was offering.

Clasping it between hers, she said warmly, 'Oh, but what a *heavenly* day! You are my *third* gift from the gods. Has Robert told you how much I love your paintings?'

'Yes, and I'm very flattered you like them, Lady Hartigan.'

Liz smiled, her manner composed. Inwardly she was in agony. How could any man *stop* loving this ravishing girl who was not only gorgeous to look at, but also exuded sweetness of character almost as palpably as she emanated a faint, delicious aroma of French scent?

'Have you only just got here, Bethany?' her husband asked, noticing the absence of a drink on the marble-topped table.

'No, I was here at twelve-thirty—you know me. But I told Mr Twomey I'd wait for you to arrive. Here he comes now,' she added, as a slimly-built good-looking man in a tailcoat and black tie approached.

He greeted Liz first, then Robert who, a few minutes later, while David was explaining his presence in London to Bethany, said to her, 'Michael Twomey has been working here since he was sixteen and I suppose he's now fifty-something, although he doesn't look it. The day he retires the Ritz will never be the same for me. I've known him since I was a small boy and came here for tea with my great-grandmother. She pre-empted pop stars in wearing dark glasses at all times. The reason was, she had ruined her eyes with belladonna which Edwardian women used to make their eyes sparkle.' Watching his face as he talked, Liz realised why he had seemed familiar. There was something about him which reminded her of the portrait of Lorenzo de' Medici in the bedroom which had been Bethany's at the Villa Delphini.

'Twomey knows all the foibles of the people who are or used to be habitués,' he went on. 'He once told me that, years ago, he used to make late-night snacks for Nubar Gulbenkian, the Armenian millionaire who rode about London in his private taxi. My great-grandmother's smoked glass spectacles made her inclined to trip on the steps over there. Whenever he saw her coming, Michael Twomey would make sure she didn't fall flat on her face. He personifies the Ritz for me. I hope he'll write his memoirs some day. They should be fascinating.'

'I've never been here before,' said Liz, her trained eye noting such details as the Greek border edging the marble floor, the intricate mouldings at the base of the columns, and the gilded dolphins and fish-tailed boys blowing small shell horns above a naked golden nymph on the other side of the Palm Court.

'Isn't it marvellously Edwardian?' said Bethany, turning to talk to her.

They were now side by side on the sofa, with the two men sitting on rather feminine French chairs which emphasised the height and breadth of shoulder common to them both.

Liz murmured agreement. It was easy to visualise the Palm Court filled with bejewelled women with pouter pigeon bosoms and sweeping trains escorted by men in white waistcoats and tails.

Bethany started to tell her about the Redwoods she owned. It was impossible not to like her.

It wasn't until they were seated at one of the window tables in the beautiful dining-room with its Boucher-blue clouded ceiling and far-apart tables that David asked, 'What was your first gift from the gods today, Bethany?'

'Oh . . .' She flashed a soft glance at her husband. 'The reason we came up today was for me to see my gynaecologist. Having Sylvie, our second baby, wasn't quite as straightforward as Tom's arrival. But I'm fine again now, thank goodness. Fit as a fiddle.'

Liz wondered if David understood the significance of this reply, and if it tore him apart to think of Robert and Bethany making love for the first time since their daughter's birth.

On Robert's recommendation, they all began lunch with oysters served on silver octagonal plates with ice and lemon. David explained he was thinking of returning to Blackmead and would value Robert's advice on the wisdom or folly of that undertaking.

Presently, while they were enjoying fillet of turbot in puff pastry with a lemon and ginger sauce, Bethany said, 'You can't pick Robert's brains in an hour or two, David. Why don't you and Liz come to Cranmer for the weekend? Then you can discuss it at leisure.'

This was after she had tactfully established that he and Liz were living together.

'Thank you, I'd like to do that, but I can't speak for Liz,' he answered.

Did that mean he would rather go to Cranmer on his own? she wondered.

Bethany said, 'You can spare a weekend, can't you, Liz? *Do* come. I know Robert's mother would love to meet you, and you would enjoy seeing her collection of antique jewels. They are nothing to do with the family jewels. Some of these she picked up for mere pence when she was a schoolgirl. In those days, apparently, one could find heavenly things for a song.'

Not without inward misgivings, Liz succumbed to her persuasion. It was settled that, instead of returning to Blackmead at the end of their time in London, she and David would drive down to Cranmer Castle.

It happened that the following weekend the young nanny who looked after Lord Lyndon—called by his mother Tom Kitten, Tompkins and other pet names— and his infant sister, had several days' leave to be a bridesmaid at her sister's wedding.

This meant Bethany was in sole charge of her children and consequently Liz saw more of them than she would had their nanny been there.

In childhood she had preferred live and toy animals to dolls. Where other people's children were concerned, she had never felt any strong urge to coo over babies or play games with small fry. Awkward teenagers she found interesting and would lend a sympathetic ear to their plans and problems. But in general she preferred the company of adults, although she had always expected to have several children of her own one day.

When, on Sunday afternoon, while they were sitting in the garden, Bethany suddenly dumped the baby in her arms while she went to the aid of her son who had fallen and hurt himself, Liz was startled to realise how much she was enjoying holding the shawl-swaddled, almost bald scrap known to the world as Lady Sylvie Rathbone.

'Thanks.'

Having kissed Tom's bumped knee better, Bethany retrieved her daughter from Liz and put her back in the refurbished old perambulator which had once been occupied by her husband.

It was clear that she adored her children, although a few minutes earlier she had confided that, having had two in quick succession, she meant now to have a long gap before, as she'd put it, 'producing my second batch.'

Now she said, 'Before I was married, I worked in a flower shop in Chelsea, but now I have to find something I can do at home. I don't want Robert to get bored with a wife whose only interests are him and his offspring, especially as I have Nanny to relieve me of all the hard part of being a mother. When I was at school I was going to base a career on languages. French was always my best subject and in Portofino I picked up Italian quite quickly. Has David told you how he rescued me from Blackmead?'

Liz shook her head. 'He did say your stepmother was unkind to you.'

'Yes, but as Madame de Staël said: To understand all is to forgive all. I didn't know at the time that my father wasn't my father. Nor did David. We both thought David was my uncle, which made it all the more complicated when I fell madly in love with him.'

A faint sound from inside the pram made her rise from the white wooden bench to peer at the baby.

Liz sat very still and tense, hoping Sylvie wasn't about to start crying, thereby putting an end to her mother's revelations.

Bethany spent a few moments watching her infant before she sat down and went on, 'David was my first love. I was brokenhearted when he sent me back to England. I thought, you see, that he loved me but wouldn't admit it because of our blood relationship and because he was so much older.'

'How did you find out you weren't related to each other?' Liz asked.

'On my twentieth birthday I was given a letter my mother had written before she died, telling me about my natural father.'

'How did David react to that?'

'We weren't in touch with each other and by then I was engaged to Robert. Later on, when I did see David again, he explained that years before, as a young man, he'd been in love with my mother. But that was more than twenty years ago, and now he has you,' said Bethany, smiling at her.

'Well . . . for the time being,' Liz answered lightly.

'Only for the time being? You seem to have so much in common . . . to be so well suited,' said the younger girl.

'We have got on well so far—yes,' Liz conceded guardedly. 'But I'm sure David would agree that our work is what matters most to us. We would both always put our work before any personal relationship.'

She adopted this attitude because although Bethany had spoken frankly and freely about her own life, Liz had no intention of confiding in her. Young wives who looked at their husbands the way Bethany looked at Robert kept nothing secret from them. If Liz confessed to being in love with David, Robert would hear about it and might drop a hint to him that women in love, who were not deeply loved in return, could quickly become an encumbrance.

At this point the two men came through the archway leading into the Castle's herb garden. With a shout, Tom rushed to his father and was scooped up and swung in the air.

Watching the man and his son, Liz was racked with longing to be like Bethany; a wife and mother with a secure, happy future. In spite of what she had said a few minutes earlier, she knew that, for her, a close loving relationship was as important as her work.

That night, in their bedroom, after a private dinner party with their weekend guests and her parents-in-law, as Bethany took off her make-up she said to her husband, 'Do you think David is in love with Liz?'

'How should I know?' Robert replied, in a tone which suggested it was a strange thing to ask.

'Did he mention her while you were out on your walk this afternoon?'

'No, we were talking about Blackmead—whether he can afford to keep the place going.'

'Does he want to?'

'If it's not going to break him—yes.'

'Which suggests he has marriage and children in mind,' said Bethany. 'I hope so. I like her enormously. What do you think of her?'

Robert, already undressed and ready for bed, was sitting in a chair by her dressing-table, reading an article in *Country Life*. Resigning himself to a discussion of their guests, he closed the magazine.

'I haven't spent as much time with her as you have. She's a good-looking girl and obviously a talented painter. She doesn't seem very forthcoming. I don't think it's shyness. If anything she strikes me as too self-possessed.'

'Only with you,' said his wife. 'And I understand that perfectly. Even though you don't look predatory nowadays—or at least not when I'm around—there's something about you which makes women put on their armour. Liz was perfectly natural and relaxed with your parents and me. It's her attitude to David which puzzles me. If one didn't know they were lovers, one would never guess it. They're not in the least demonstrative with each other.'

'Nor are we . . . by day.' Robert watched his wife let down her long lustrous hair which had been pinned up for dinner.

'No, but we do exchange looks,' she replied, as the thick swathes slipped down to her shoulders. 'David and Liz don't even seem to do that. When I was talking to her in the herb garden this afternoon, she spoke as if their relationship were only a temporary thing.'

'She must be getting on for thirty. Perhaps there's a husband in the background,' Robert suggested.

'She's twenty-eight and she's never been married—I asked her. But obviously there have been other men in her life. She's too attractive not to have had other lovers.'

'Are you beginning to regret that you've had only one?' he enquired, the question accompanied by the faint enigmatic smile which she thought of as his Lorenzo look.

'Not for a second,' she assured him. 'I have enough sense to know that very few men are as wonderful in bed as you are, my darling.'

'If any,' said Robert gravely. Then he laughed, and a single lithe movement brought him from the chair to the wide-topped Chippendale stool on which she was sitting. 'If you really believe that statement and are not just buttering my ego, why aren't we in bed?' he murmured, putting one arm round her waist.

She leaned against his broad shoulder. 'Darling, do you think David can *still* be carrying a torch for my mother? I remember that day at Portofino when it all came right between us, between you and me, David told me my mother had been the other half of him . . . that he could never forget her . . . never really love anyone else. But it was such aeons ago. Surely the ghost of a woman who died when he was in his twenties can't go on haunting him for ever?'

It was Robert Rathbone's opinion—one of the few he had never shared with his wife—that David had lied to Bethany on that memorable day at Portofino.

The full story of David's youthful infatuation with his brother's first wife, which might well have developed into an adulterous affair if her justifiably jealous husband hadn't sent David packing, was known to the whole Rathbone family; as was the fact that Clare Castle had later had an illicit affair with a violinist, Benedict Laurence, who had been Bethany's father.

It was Bethany's physical likeness to her mother, and the knowledge that she hadn't replaced Clare Castle in John Castle's heart—in spite of what his first wife had made him suffer—which had made Margaret Castle a captious, ungenerous stepmother.

Robert was deeply grateful to the man who had removed the sixteen-year-old Bethany from her unhappy home at Blackmead. He was also convinced that David had fallen in love with her during the time she was in his care. The story that he was still in love with her mother was, thought Robert, one he had invented on finding he had lost her to a younger man.

As clearly as his wife did, Robert remembered the day he and David, together, had flown from London to join her at the Villa Delphini. Although at the time

While they waited for it, he said, 'Robert has encouraged me to think I can keep this place up without bankrupting myself. But how do you feel about living here instead of in Italy?'

It was a difficult question to answer. She had thought he would make the decision without reference to her.

After prolonged hesitation, she said, 'Would you have to give up the villa if you lived here?'

'Not necessarily. Why do you ask?'

'It's such a beautiful house. If I were you, I couldn't bear to part with it—even for my ancestral home. I've no doubt this house could be lovely if someone like David Mlinaric were given a free hand. But it does need an awful lot doing—except for this room. This is perfect as it is.'

She looked round the high-ceilinged library, its walls lined with thousands of volumes in the worn leather bindings which gave the room its distinctive and, to her, delicious smell.

Most of the Castles had been outdoor people, happier on horseback or with a gun over their arm than in intellectual pursuits. But in the years when the house was new there had been one Castle who, perhaps merely as a status symbol, had added the library wing and chosen the books to fill it. Now, in the present generation, there was David who, if he lived here, would have the family portraits and other oil paintings cleaned, and introduce contemporary artists.

'I can't afford the services of a top designer. I'll have to rely on my own taste and make changes piecemeal, not all at once,' he answered. 'I take it you're not very keen to take a hand in it with me?'

'Of course I will help you—as long as I'm with you,' she added. 'But I must admit I prefer your Italian lifestyle. Don't you miss the pool and the view and dinner at Luigi's?'

'Yes, I do,' he agreed, with a frown. 'But one can't have everything in life. Here there are other things I like.'

I don't know what they can be that you can't have or do in Italy, Liz was thinking, as tea arrived.

If he hadn't spoken fluent Italian, or if he had been a writer instead of an artist and had needed to be near reference libraries and record archives, she could have understood his desire to return to England. As it was, the only reason for returning which seemed at all logical to her was a feeling of obligation to perpetuate his family line.

But the woman he wanted was forever out of reach and Liz knew that, even if he asked her to marry him, she could never say yes to a proposal made only because he wanted heirs and someone to help him do up the house.

Much as she loved him, she could never marry a man who didn't want her and love her for herself alone.

In the days that followed her spirits sank lower and lower.

The unappetising food and having Margaret Castle at the table with them made meals—always a pleasure in Italy—times of day she wished she could skip.

The weather was variable. When it wasn't fine, the clouds and the grey light depressed her. She missed Portofino.

One day, when David was going to be busy all morning going round the house and its outbuildings with a surveyor to find out the structural condition, she borrowed the car and drove to Coventry to see the Sutherland tapestry.

Looking at one of his masterworks reminded her of being told that Graham Sutherland and his wife Katharine had first met at art school when he was seventeen and she two years younger. Seven years later they had married and begun a life of rare happiness, much of it spent at the Villa Blanche high in the hills behind Menton on the Côte d'Azur. Liz had heard that, when he became a famous painter, Sutherland had insisted his wife should be dressed by Saint Laurent and had bought her romantic presents such as yards of antique Venetian silk for the walls of her bedroom.

It depressed Liz to think that the same kind of sun-filled, carefree Mediterranean life would have been possible for David and herself if it hadn't been for Blackmead and Bethany.

A few days later she went on another expedition, this time to Woburn Abbey, the palatial seat of the Dukes of Bedford.

She had hoped David would want to go with her to see the Abbey's art treasures. However, he said rather curtly that he was too busy at Blackmead to have time to look at other houses, although she was welcome to go if she could afford a day off.

This ill-chosen remark—she was already worriedly aware how little work she had accomplished since coming to England—had sparked a heated exchange which had ended with him tossing the car keys on to a table and leaving the room.

By the time she arrived at Woburn, Liz's anger had cooled, leaving her depressingly conscious of how, almost day by day, their relationship seemed to be deteriorating. It was almost as if at the Villa Delphini they had been two different people.

CHAPTER SIX

BY mid-afternoon Liz was on her way back from Woburn, her pleasure in all she had seen there diminished by not having David beside her to discuss the great house and its treasures.

On reaching the Manor, she left the car in the stable-yard and rushed into the house, eager to make up their tiff.

'Do you know where Sir David is, Nanny?' she asked, encountering Miss Evans.

'I couldn't say, Miss Redwood. I haven't seen him since lunch.'

A search of the house and garden was unsuccessful. Deflated, she returned indoors and went up to their room.

Lying on the bed, wondering where he had gone—not far without the car—and when he would come back, she felt her eyelids drooping. Normally she never slept during the day, but the wakeful nights at Cranmer were catching up with her.

She was roused from a nap by footsteps and the creaking floorboards midway from the door to the bathroom door.

'David!' A little woolly from the sudden awakening, but not too confused to remember she wanted to make up, she held her arms out to him.

He didn't ignore the conciliatory gesture. But he didn't smile as he said, 'I've been sweating. I need a bath.'

Sweaty or not, he could have given me a friendly

peck, just to show willing, Liz thought, as the door closed behind him.

He hadn't wanted to. Why? Because he was still in a huff from their row this morning? Because he was in a new huff, having found he wanted the car after she had taken it? Or—most chilling thought of all— because he was going off her?

Oh, no, here we go again, she thought, in despair. *Why* do I let my life get into these messes? I could survive what went wrong with Barney and Richard. It was upsetting, but it wasn't the end of the world.

This thing with David is different. I love him more deeply, more completely. If we break up, my heart will break.

She was curled on the window seat, filing her nails with an emery board, when he reappeared, a towel wrapped round his hips.

'How was Woburn?' he asked.

'Interesting. What have you been doing to work up a sweat?'

'Running a few miles. Without the pool I'm beginning to get out of shape.'

'You look in great shape to me, but I know what you mean. I need exercise too. For days when it's too wet to run, you could turn one of the outbuildings into a gym,' she suggested. 'It shouldn't cost a fortune.'

'Not a bad idea,' he agreed.

Although they were making conversation, it wasn't the easy spontaneous flow of talk they shared normally. This morning's near-quarrel was still lurking under the surface like a crocodile in a muddy river, waiting for one of them to rock the boat.

David had brought some bottles of wine from Italy and was keeping them in the wardrobe.

He said, 'I'm going to have a drink. Is it too early for you?'

'No, I'd love one.'

He never went anywhere without his Swiss Army knife which had a corkscrew. To make less work for Miss Evans, he and Liz made their bed. But every day Nanny changed the water in the bedside carafe which had an upturned glass to cover it and another standing beside it. A few moments later he brought her a tumbler of wine and sat down on the other side of the window seat.

'*Alla salute*,' he said, before tasting the wine.

'*Alla salute*,' she echoed.

'I've been thinking things over,' he said. 'Perhaps I can afford to have the place done up professionally. There are one or two pieces of furniture and porcelain which should fetch enough at auction to pay Mlinaric's fee for redesigning the principal rooms.'

'Oh, but why sell your family treasures? You have excellent taste. You don't really need a designer. I——'

He cut off her offer to help. 'Yes, I could do it myself, but it would take time and energy I can't spare,' he answered briskly. 'After you'd gone, I telephoned Cranmer to get Mlinaric's number. I knew they would have it—he's worked there. He wasn't in when I called, but he's going to ring back.'

To whom had he spoken? Liz wondered. To Bethany? Had asking for the designer's number, which he could have got from directory enquiries, been merely an excuse to speak to her? She was another man's wife, but so had been her mother, Clare Castle, and that hadn't stopped him falling in love with her.

Perhaps wanting unobtainable women was a thing with him, she thought unhappily. Something to do with forbidden fruit being the sweetest.

Having skipped lunch and had only two biscuits to eat since a light breakfast, she could feel the wine going to her head. Perhaps it would give her the nerve to say, Don't waste your life wanting someone you can never have . . . someone who doesn't love you. Take what's on offer—me.

But as she gulped some more wine, David rose and reached for her glass which he placed on the sill with his own.

'You can finish that later,' he said, as he pulled her to her feet and into his arms.

Half an hour later she knew that what had just happened hadn't restored the rapport they had had at Portofino.

Even the way he made love was different since going to Cranmer. He had taken her with a fierce, greedy sensuality, but without any tenderness. There had been none of the caresses which had characterised his lovemaking in Italy. He had not brushed his lips from the blue veins inside her wrists to the tender pulse-points of her elbows, or nibbled her ears or feathered his fingers down her spine.

From the first rough, lascivious kiss to the final triumphant thrust, he had made her feel there was nothing but sex between them. An impression reinforced when, without any gentle after-play, he rose from her hot, damp body and flung himself on to his back, his deep chest still rising and falling from the recent exertion.

He had stayed there only a few moments before swinging himself off the bed and going back to the bathroom.

Now, as she watched him replenish the glasses and bring one of them to her, Liz realised how little satisfaction there was in an act of love when it was only an expression of physical desire. Her body felt good, but her mind was still tense and troubled.

'Thank you.'

As he placed her glass on the night table, she pushed herself up on her elbows preparatory to sitting up. The action thrust out her breasts now glazed by a sheen of moisture, partly from her own pores and partly from his lips and tongue.

On many occasions at the villa, the sight of her glistening breasts after they had made love had caused him to press a soft kiss on each swollen point. It had been a loving gesture which had never failed to touch her deeply. But he did not make it today. Perhaps he never would again. Something had left their relationship ... or someone had intervened.

For ten days after going to Woburn, Liz tried to convince herself that things would come right between them. She knew in her heart they wouldn't, any more than the leaves of autumn could regain the soft greens of spring.

Her Italian summer was over and, with it, the love of her life. David was unquestionably the right man, the perfect man for *her*. But she wasn't the right one for him.

Having accepted that fact, she saw no point in prolonging the agony. While she was shut in the library, supposedly painting, she composed a letter of farewell.

David,

Our summer at Portofino will be one of my life's happiest memories, but the time has come to say goodbye. I think what you need from now on is not a girl-friend but a wife. I'm sure it won't be too hard to find someone who has grown up in a house like Blackmead and who will enjoy being 'the lady of the manor'. Where my future lies, I don't know. Perhaps nowhere permanently. As you once said, the world is full of wonders and it seems a pity not to see as many as possible. I am grateful for the good times we've had together. I'm leaving you one of my paintings as a memento.   Liz.

Next morning, while David and Margaret were both out, she packed her belongings and caught the eleven o'clock bus which passed the gates of the Manor on its way to Northampton. From there she rang Jane to tell her she was coming to London and to warn her agent that, if she had a call from David, she wasn't on any account to reveal Liz's lease of the flat.

'Okay, but what's this all about? Don't tell me it's over already?'

'It's over,' said Liz. 'I can't talk now. I'll call you later. Goodbye.'

As she replaced the receiver, the pain became overwhelming. Tears squeezed between her closed eyelids. She hunched her shoulders and crossed her arms round her ribcage, trying to contain the explosive pressure of sobs building up inside her.

Someone tapped on the glass with the edge of a coin. Somehow she managed to pull herself together.

'Are you all right, miss?' the man who was waiting asked, when he saw her face.

She nodded and hurried away. But she wasn't all right and she didn't think she ever would be.

'He rang an hour after you did,' said Jane, at the flat that evening.

Liz said, 'If you let him know where I am, Jane, I'll find myself another agent. I mean that. I don't want to talk to him on the telephone, or see him, or have anything more to do with him. Please give me your solemn promise you'll tell him absolutely nothing. Say I've gone abroad and left no forwarding address.'

'If you're sure that's the way you want it,' her friend agreed, looking concerned. 'What did he *do*, for God's sake? It isn't that long since you were looking as happy as I've ever seen you.'

'Don't be offended, but I don't want to talk about it. Not yet. Not for a long time.'

The days that followed were a repetition of the period following her father's death. Only then she had been mourning the past. Now she was mourning the future.

A future which, as it said in *The Times* when a wedding was cancelled, would not now take place.

If she hadn't been so unhappy, Lambert's flat in Chelsea would have been a delight. It consisted of a large studio with a tiny kitchen and bathroom and a small terrace. It was decorated with the unerring taste of an artistic homosexual.

For several days she didn't go out. She lived on oranges and yoghurt and stayed in bed or lay on the sofa, thinking about the way things might have been. She spent a lot of time crying.

The prospect of life without David—perhaps forty or fifty years of it—was so unutterably dreary she could understand why some people committed suicide. But she wasn't one of them. Having seen her father and other patients at the hospice dying when they didn't want to, she could never throw away her life. Besides, she still had her work. Mingled with the despair was the knowledge that it would get better. Slowly, the misery would lessen and then she would start to work again. That alone would make life worth living.

Presently, she began to go out for long walks. At first she walked to tire herself out and help her to sleep at night, not taking any interest in the buildings or the people she passed.

Combined with her lack of appetite, the hours of walking made her lose weight. Because she still had a tan being thinner didn't make her look ill, it merely emphasised what David had called her bone-deep beauty. Many times, after making love, he had lain beside her, propped on one elbow, while his finger outlined her cheekbones, the edge of bone marked by her eyebrows and the clean line from ear to chin. She had only to close her eyes to recall his light touch on her face; that, and much, much else it would be better to forget, at least for the next year or two.

Perhaps there would come a time when she could enjoy those memories. At the moment they filled her with pain, making her long for a pill which would induce temporary amnesia and blot out all recollection of the immediate past.

A week after Liz's arrival in London, Jane and her husband went on holiday for three weeks. At the time of her departure Jane hadn't received any more telephone calls from David. No doubt, after the first shock of finding Liz gone, he had seen her abrupt departure as the best way to end their affair.

It was a beautiful autumn. Day after day of blue skies and mellow sunshine. Fallen leaves lay in golden drifts along the side streets and squares of Chelsea and South Kensington.

Although for a time the trauma of leaving Blackmead had deadened her normal reactions, gradually ten years of being a practising artist, and a lifetime of having an observant curiosity, made her start to take notice again. The woman continued to suffer; the artist had begun to recover.

It was warm enough to sit on benches, sketching people, architectural details, cats and dogs, anything which caught her eye.

One day she had a bad fright when, walking along Fulham Road, she heard a man's voice shout 'Liz!'

For an instant she thought it was David and was struck by terror and joy. Her head had dreaded a chance encounter with him; her undisciplined heart longed for it.

The man on the opposite pavement who had called to her wasn't David. At first she didn't recognise him. There was something vaguely familiar about the way he dashed across the road, making the driver of a car give an angry blast on his horn.

But even when he reached her side and said, 'It *is* you. I wasn't absolutely certain. Liz, don't you know me?' she continued to be baffled.

Because she was still in shock from thinking she had run into David, it took her a few seconds more to make sense of a voice she knew and a familiar pair of smiling hazel eyes when the man confronting her was a stranger.

Then she realised who he was. Her first smile since coming to London lit up her face.

'*Barney!* My goodness, how you've changed. If you'd been on this side of the street, I'd have walked straight past you.''

'You've changed quite a lot yourself. But I recognised those great legs. It's great to see you. For old times' sake, can we hug?'

'Of course.'

She opened her arms and they gave each other a bear-hug.

'I still can't believe my eyes,' Liz told him, a short time later, when they were having coffee in a nearby café. 'You're just not recognisable as the shaggy-haired, bearded rebel in way-out clothes I've been remembering all these years. When did this spruce, suave man about town break out from that wild woolly chrysalis?'

He grinned at her. 'When did the kid with lilac hair and crazy make-up turn into the gorgeous creature I'm looking at now? We grew up, Liz. You made your name as a painter and I, like hundreds of others, had to face up to the fact that I wasn't ever going to make it as a "great artist" but I could earn a pretty good living as a graphics designer.'

It took them half an hour to bring each other up to date with the main events of their lives in the years since their youthful romance. Barney, she discovered, was now the father of two young children, but divorced from their mother. Liz told him only that she had had one long relationship but was now on her own again.

'Look, I have to go now, but is there any chance that you've a free evening in the not too distant future?' he asked. 'Could we have dinner? We still have a lot to talk about.'

'I'd like that, Barney. I have every night free from now until kingdom come. Pick whichever suits you.'

He looked surprised. 'Let's make it tonight, then.'

Later, taking trouble with her appearance for the first time since leaving Blackmead, she wondered if it had been a mistake to let Barney know she was a single again. Perhaps he'd expect to end the evening in bed with her. But that side of life was over for her. Loving David, she could never make love with anyone else. Although in his new persona Barney was even more attractive than the unkempt but dishy student who had been her first love, she was in no mood to resume their relationship. Before he wined and dined her she had better make that clear. It wasn't fair to encourage expectations which weren't going to be fulfilled.

When he arrived at the flat, which he thought was her own until she explained about Lambert, she offered him a choice of beer, gin or wine. She had bought the drinks that afternoon, and some things to nibble and two flowering pot plants. It was another small advance in the direction of becoming a fully functioning person again.

As she handed him the beer he had asked for, she said, 'Barney, may I be blunt? I'm alone and I'm lonely. But I only need friendship. Anything more is a no-go area.'

There was a pause before he answered, 'All right, Liz. If that's how you want it. I won't deny that, if you'd been willing, I shouldn't have been averse to making a night of it. But I can take no for an answer without getting sulky—even when the answer comes before the question,' he added, with dry humour which reminded her painfully of David.

Another reminder of David was being taken to Gavvers in Lower Sloane Street. This restaurant was also owned by the Roux brothers, but it catered to a less affluent clientele with a fixed price menu which included coffee and wine but gave a more limited choice of dishes than Le Gavroche.

'Although I've been told the food here is often just as good as it is at their three-star place,' said Barney, after they had been shown to a table within inches of its neighbours.

The restaurant was staffed by young girls with friendly smiles and most of the patrons were young. Lively conversations at the tables on either side of theirs made it possible for Barney to confide the history of his broken marriage.

'I guess I married Elaine on the rebound from you, which was a stupid thing to do. It was okay for six months, by which time she was pregnant. Then we began to realise we had nothing in common. We were trying to make the best of things, which is why she got pregnant the second time, when she met her ideal man. He was willing to take on the kids and I couldn't see the point of all three of us being fed up, so we had an amicable divorce.'

He paused to drink some white wine before going on, 'I see my two kids regularly but, if I'm honest, I can't say they're that important to me. Elaine was the one who wanted them. Being the mum whose kids have the whitest T-shirts and a kitchen floor you can eat off are her two main reasons for living. Tim is her male opposite number, the sort who spends all day Sunday washing the car and mowing his billiard-table lawn. I prefer reading the papers. I may have got my exterior a bit more together, but I'm still the same slob inside.'

'Not quite the same,' Liz remarked. 'I can remember the time when you would have murdered your wife for looking at another man.'

He nodded. 'If I hadn't been so bloody jealous you and I might still be together. I knew I was turning you off, but I couldn't help it. I suppose it was because I never had anyone who belonged to me. I was terrified of losing you. You see, all that stuff I told you about my family was a lie. My family consisted of thirty other kids and the staff who were paid to look after us.'

'You mean you grew up in an orphanage?'

'That's right. Where we had plenty to eat and were treated a great deal better than kids with two lousy parents. It was a good place to grow up, except that everything was shared. I wanted things of my own. That's why I didn't like it when you had other friends. I wanted you to be *mine*.'

'Which I was—then,' she said gently. 'Why didn't you tell me, Barney? Surely you didn't think it would put me off you?'

'Not really. My common sense told me you wouldn't give a damn. But I thought your family might not like it. You never talked much about your background, but I knew it was different from most people's. Upper crust. I couldn't see your father being keen on a son-in-law who didn't know who his parents were. That was another of my hang-ups. While most of the guys only wanted to make it with as many girls as possible, I was keen to start playing house. Crazy, but that's what I wanted. That's why I married Elaine.'

'I wish you'd told me,' she said.

She understood now something which had always puzzled her; Barney's unusual concern that she shouldn't get pregnant. From what other girls had told her, most boys couldn't care less. Girls had the pill to protect them. If they didn't want to take it, that was their look-out. If something went wrong, a nice boy would share the expense of having it put right. But most of them took the attitude that it was up to the girls what happened to their bodies.

Barney hadn't been like that. At last she understood his unusual care and caution. Unlike his own male parent, he wasn't going to sire a child until he was ready to be a father to it.

'How little we really know about people we think we know well,' said Liz. 'I must have been pretty stupid when I was eighteen. I should have guessed there had to be some special reason why you were the way you were. Ten years ago. Doesn't it sound a *long* time! It seems to have gone in a flash.'

And ten years from now, where shall I be then? Liz thought bleakly. Still on my own? Still longing for David?

They walked back to her flat where she said, 'I won't ask you in for a nightcap, but how about coming to supper on Thursday night? I'm a pretty good cook now.'

'I'll look forward to it.'

'Thank you for a nice evening, Barney. I'm glad we've met again.'

'So am I. Goodnight, kitten.'

The kiss he dropped on her cheek was no more than a friendly peck; the kind of social salute older generations gave each other all the time. It was his use of the pet name from ten years ago which bothered her slightly as she got ready for bed.

She had told him, in bald outline, about her three years with Richard. She hadn't mentioned David. Perhaps, on Thursday, she should say something. Barney was also lonely. Since his divorce there had been no woman in his life. There might have been several with whom he had had one-night stands; but none who had meant anything to him. He was ripe for a more satisfying relationship. She didn't want him to start thinking they could rekindle an old flame.

She had never forgotten Barney because he had been her first love. But she was a different person from the girl he remembered. All they had in common now was 'remembrance of things past'. It was a good basis for friendship. Not for marriage.

Also, her instinct told her he wouldn't find it easy to cope with a woman who earned more than he did, or who was in any way more successful. Once or twice during the evening he had made remarks about the company he worked for which had suggested that he didn't think women were fitted to be top executives. Up to a certain level, fine. But certainly not quite up to and never superior to senior males.

One of the things about David that had made her love him was that, in spite of his jokey attitude to aggressive feminism, in his general outlook he made no distinctions between men and women. People were gifted, hard-working, good value—a favourite term of praise with him—or they were not.

She didn't know—perhaps one day she would ask Barney—but she thought it likely that of the two parents who hadn't wanted or been able to rear him, he felt more resentment towards his mother.

Thinking about unwanted children made her wish she were carrying David's baby. She could afford to support a child and the nature of her work would have made it easy to combine her career with motherhood.

David's daughter: a tall honey-blonde child with his cobalt eyes to whom Liz could have been the kind of mother she herself had always longed for. Firm when it mattered. Easygoing when it didn't.

God, what a fool she had been, when she realised he didn't want marriage, not to make sure she got pregnant. A child of her love for him would have made all the difference to her lonely future.

Too late now, she thought forlornly.

Later on Sunday night, Jane, back from holiday, called her. She had been hoping that during her absence Liz and David would have got together. Liz told her firmly there was no possibility of a reconciliation.

'How about lunch tomorrow?' Jane suggested.

They arranged to meet at The Picnic Basket.

Next morning, soon after ten, Jane telephoned again.

'Guess who was camped on my doorstep when I got to the office? David Warren. He's *determined* to find out where you are. I don't think he believes I don't know.'

Liz's heart beat a wild tattoo. David in London, looking for her!

'Did he say why he wanted to see me?'

'No, only that it was urgent. I must say he looks like a man with something important on his mind. You can see he hasn't been sleeping well. I think you should see him, honey. He wants you back. He's missing you.'

'Probably he is,' said Liz. 'People who are used to electric blankets find beds cold without them. I don't want to go back on the only terms he can offer. You gave me your sworn promise, Jane. Don't let me down.'

'Oh, okay, if you insist,' her agent agreed reluctantly. 'We'll talk about it over lunch. If you want me to go on lying for you, you might at least tell what went wrong.'

'If you don't mind I'll take a raincheck on lunch. If David's in London I'd rather stay close to my burrow. You must have a million things to do, your first day back. I'm sure you'll be glad to send out for a sandwich. We can get together in a few days. Thanks for calling, Jane. 'Bye.'

Before the American could argue, Liz rang off.

She was jumpy for the rest of the day. When, after lunch, the bell rang, she was half afraid to answer it in case she found David on *her* doorstep. But there was no way he could find her except through Jane, who wasn't a person to go back on her word.

The caller turned out to be a man delivering the boxes she'd had in storage but which she had only recently bothered to send for.

But for Jane's upsetting call, she would have derived some pleasure from unpacking belongings she hadn't seen for a long time. Now her interest in them was swamped by a consuming curiosity to know why David wanted to see her.

Could he be piqued by her walking out on him? Richard had been angry enough to take it out on Jane. But David was a larger man than Richard, not only in the physical sense. She couldn't believe his reason for wanting to see her was merely to blast her for daring to take the initiative in bringing their affair to an end.

All day and half the night she thought of possible reasons why David wanted to see her.

The one put forward by her heart—that after she had left him he had found he needed her, loved her—was at once rejected by her intellect as inadmissible wishful thinking.

The next day she was surprised to receive a visit from Gil, Jane's husband.

Because of Liz's enthusiasm for the area, the Adams had spent their vacation in Andalusia, exploring old towns such as Ronda and Arcos de la Frontera. They had also spent a day in Tangier on the other side of the strait which separated North Africa from southern Europe. Gil's call seemed at first to be to deliver a caftan Jane had bought for Liz in the casbah.

'The reason I brought the caftan to you is that Jane is worried that your ex-friend Warren is having her watched in the hope she'll lead him to you,' he said, after some conversation about their holiday.

'What! That would be crazy,' Liz expostulated.

'She says he looks a bit crazy. That's not why you split up, is it? Because he's unbalanced?'

'No, no—he's as sane as you, Gil. I can't believe he would go to such lengths. He has no reason to think I'm in London. The most likely place for me to be is on one of the Greek islands. They were where I was planning to go after Italy. Look, if you're worried that he might attack Jane, or become abusive, don't be. He's not a violent man.'

'I'm not concerned about that. Jane says he's extremely polite. But she's never been a good liar and she thinks *he* knows she does know where you are and is determined to worm it out of her.'

'In that case, if he goes on pestering, she'd better tell him she's received my address and will forward a letter. But I won't see him, Gil. I can't. It's almost a month now since I left him and I'm only just beginning to feel human and not like a zombie. I've been through hell, and I can't take any more.'

Her voice wobbled on the last words. Her eyes filled with tears.

'You see what I mean,' she said in a strangled croak as she jumped up to find a tissue.

Gil Adams was a kind, sensible man who could take a few tears in his stride. They had been drinking tea. Now he went across to the drinks tray and poured out two gin and tonics.

Handing one of them to her, he said, 'Jane and I are very fond of you, Liz. We hate to see you unhappy. Ordinarily we shouldn't pry into your private life. But as Jane is go-between in this situation, I think she's entitled to know your reason for leaving Warren. If she knew he'd treated you badly in some way, it would make it easier for her to deal with him.'

Liz could well understand how, if David exerted himself, he could make Jane inclined to sympathise. She wanted to tell Gil the truth, but instinct told her that if he and Jane knew she loved David, they would think they had only to bring the two of them together for everything to sort itself out. Instead of which they would be exposing her to the torment of seeing him again.

'I'm sorry, Gil,' she answered. 'It's too personal . . . too private . . . something I can't discuss even with my closest friends. Just believe me when I say I don't want to see him again—ever. Maybe I should go abroad. Then Jane could tell him the truth.'

He had seen how much thinner she was, how drained of the vibrant vitality which had always been

part of her attractiveness. She looked like someone
after a bad bout of 'flu; washed out, easily upset, not
fit to travel anywhere.

'No, I don't think that's necessary,' he said. 'Jane
can cope. She's quite a tough cookie. You can talk to
each other by telephone until she feels sure the coast is
clear, as it were.'

On Wednesday, Liz rang Jane. A letter of thanks for
the caftan was already in the post.

'Yes, Mr Warren has been to see me today, but he
didn't stay long,' said Jane. 'I told him the best thing
to do was to write to you. If he does, I'll have the
letter brought to you by motorbike messenger.'

Liz spent most of Thursday preparing the meal for
Barney. She was trying not to let herself live for the
moment when David's letter came. She knew it was
madness to suppose it would make an iota of
difference to the status quo, yet she couldn't help
endlessly wondering what it was he had to say to her.

Barney arrived with a four-ounce vacuum-packed
jar of pasteurised Sevruga caviar and a bottle of vodka.
They put the jar on crushed ice and the vodka in the
freezer while Liz made some very thin toast. Normally
she didn't eat butter, but had bought some in case he
liked it.

They shared the whole jar of tiny, grey, rich-tasting
grains, piling them on buttered toast, accompanied by
the chilled vodka.

She was on her way to the kitchen to attend to the
supper when the bell rang. Wondering if, at this hour,
it could be the messenger with David's letter, she
hurried to the door.

'Good evening, Liz,' said David. 'May I come in?'

She should have felt shocked and betrayed. Instead

she felt faint with joy. How haggard he looked, how tired. As if he had been through hell too.

Without waiting for her reply, David crossed the threshold. Liz had the impression that if she hadn't stepped back he would have brushed her aside.

The flat had no closed off hall, merely a space defined by a lower ceiling than that of the main living area and a painted archway between them.

Under the arch David paused, taking in the large comfortable room skilfully lit by table lamps, downlighters and, above the round dining table, a low hanging lamp casting a pool of soft brilliance on the two place settings.

Barney had risen from the sofa, his expression betraying his displeasure at this intrusion.

David swung to face Liz, his eyes blazing. 'It didn't take you long to find consolation,' he said savagely.

She stiffened defensively. 'You're quite mistaken. This is a very old friend from my art school days. Barney Lucas ... David Warren.'

The two men looked at each other with thinly veiled antagonism. Neither made any attempt to shake hands.

'I'm sorry to break up the party,' David said curtly. 'But I want to talk to Liz—alone,' he added pointedly.

'Now hang on there, Warren, you can't come bursting in here——'

Barney's show of authority collapsed as the other man moved towards him, his whole bearing taut with menace.

'David, please ...' Liz intervened. 'There's no need to be so aggressive.'

He ignored her. 'Get out of here,' he said softly.

Not surprisingly, Barney looked nervous.

She said hurriedly, 'I'm terribly sorry about this, but I think you had better go.'

For a moment or two he wavered, visibly torn

between outrage and the recognition that the other man was in a dangerous mood.

Scowling, he made for the hall, pausing beside Liz to ask, 'Are you sure you'll be all right?'

She nodded. 'I'll call you.'

'Don't bother to see me out.' Under the sarcasm there was anger and humiliation.

'David, that was abominable!' she exclaimed, when they were alone.

'No more abominable than walking out on me.' He glared at her, the muscles of his jaw knotted under the still sunburned skin.

'Is that why you're here? To avenge your wounded male pride? Men have been walking out on women since time began.'

It wasn't what she wanted to say. In the grip of conflicting emotions—delight at his presence, indignation at his behaviour—she maintained a defensive stance.

An enraged flush darkened his tan. His blue eyes glittered with fury. He grabbed her roughly by the shoulders, steered her backwards towards a chair and pushed her into it.

Then, with his clenched fists on his hips, looming over her, glowering, he said harshly, 'I managed to persuade your agent to tell me where I could find you by convincing her that I loved you and wanted to marry you. When she asked if I'd told you that, I said, no, I hadn't. You can't tell a woman you love her if the two of you want different things. I've been single long enough—too long. I want a wife and children, but, as you've made quite clear, you want to be free of all ties except for your work. Well, I didn't need you or even want you to wait on me. All I wanted from you was commitment: the belief that we could share our lives, pool our resources and draw comfort and strength from each other. Because that's what marriage is about when it's between grown-up people who know who they are and what they want out of life. If you'd shown the smallest sign of being ready to commit yourself, I should have asked you to marry me. But ever since we left Italy, I felt you drawing away from me. I don't really know why I'm here, except that I had to see you again ... to have one last try to get through to you.'

His outburst concluded, he flung himself down on the sofa and pressed the tips of his fingers over his eyes in the gesture of a man who has been for too long under pressure and has reached the point of having spent all his vitality. It could even be there were tears behind his closed eyelids. Certainly there were tears in her eyes when he reached the end of his tirade.

Liz rose from where he had put her and went to where he had slumped down, perching on the edge of the cushions close to his long left thigh.

With a tentative touch on his knee, she said, in a low voice, 'I thought you were still in love with Bethany. That's the real reason I left you. I couldn't bear loving *you* while you were longing for *her*.'

David's fingertips slid down his cheeks. His look of dumbfounded amazement convinced her, before he spoke, that her supposition had been mistaken. With a great weight lifted from her heart, she waited for him to confirm it.

After a pause, he said quietly, 'For a while, a long time ago, I did love Bethany—yes. No man, if he's normal, reaches my age without loving several women. But loving and marrying don't always go together. Bethany was years too young for me and what she felt didn't last long. Now would you please repeat what you said a moment ago ... about loving me.'

'I've loved you for ages but I didn't dare show it. Oh, David . . . hold me.'

She threw herself into his arms.

Later, by which time the chicken casserole Liz had left in a low oven was overcooked but still edible, David took Barney's place at the supper table.

'Suddenly I'm starving,' he told her. 'Last night your friends Jane and Gil gave me an excellent dinner at their house at Highgate, but it might as well have been sawdust.'

'If they told you last night where I was, how come it took you twenty-four hours to get here?'

'They didn't. They said I must write to you. I said it wasn't possible to write what I wanted to say. Jane was obviously worried about breaking her promise to you. But this evening she rang up the Overseas League where I'm staying and said she'd decided to back her hunch that you loved me, even if it meant you could never trust her again.'

'Thank God she did,' said Liz, with feeling. 'I must call her and tell her it's all right. I'd better do it now and put her out of her suspense.'

'Telephone her tomorrow,' said David, placing a restraining hand on her arm when she would have risen from the table. 'I told her if she hadn't heard from me within two hours of her call, she could take it I'd be spending the night here. Not that I was too confident, even though they'd both told me you were obviously unhappy.'

'What I don't understand,' said Liz, 'is why, if it had nothing to do with Bethany, after that weekend at Cranmer your whole manner became quite different. You even stopped wanting to make love as often as before.'

'Seeing Bethany and Robert so happy together, and

enjoying their children, made me realise how poorly our relationship compared with theirs,' David explained. 'Even making love lost its edge with the words missing. You did once call me darling, I remember, and I thought that was a good sign. But one isolated darling isn't very sustaining to a man who's starving to hear all the things you told me just now.' He gave a nod at the sofa.

'I was starving too,' she said lovingly. 'David, when did you *know*? When were you certain you loved me?'

'The day you didn't turn up for tea at Fortnum's. At first I was worried in case you'd walked under a bus. Then I began to wonder if you might have run across Richard and he was trying to get you to go back to him. I knew if you'd spent three years together, you must have cared a lot for him.'

She shook her head. 'Loving you has made me realise how little I cared for him.'

Later, discussing wedding plans and the future, David said, 'I know you have doubts about living in England, at Blackmead, but perhaps we can reach a compromise. Summers and Christmasses at Blackmead, but most of the winter and spring and autumn at Portofino. How would that suit you?'

'It sounds wonderful—but expensive. Could we afford it?'

'If your Casimir books are a hit and my next show of pictures goes well, I think we might.'

The next exhibition, in London, of paintings by David Warren took place the following spring and was not only praised, particularly for the Australian pictures, by the serious art critics, but was also reported in the tabloids.

The focus of their attention was *Girl In a Golden Bed*, a full-length portrait of the artist's wife.

Bethany's husband was out of England, attending an international seminar on new farming methods, at the time of the private view. He heard about it from her, and about the *succès de scandale*, when he returned to Cranmer. A few days later they went to London together so that he could see the famous portrait and the rest of the show.

Most of the paintings had sold at the private view and now all had red stars on them. *Girl In a Golden Bed* was marked in the catalogue, Not For Sale.

As they left the gallery and walked in the direction of the Ritz, Bethany said, 'If you were an artist and had painted that portrait of me, would you want other people to see it?'

Robert considered. 'I think so, yes,' he said, at length. 'It's undoubtedly David's masterpiece; the painting with which he'll be most closely identified for the rest of his life and after his death. I believe it's the closest to greatness he'll ever come. Liz didn't mind it being included in the show, did she?'

'No, I don't think so. She's too ecstatically happy to mind about anything at the moment. But I think *I* should find it unnerving to have everyone we know knowing what I look like without a stitch on. On the other hand, she is so beautiful, lying on her back with the sheets wildly rumpled and that sleepy half-smile on her face, that the picture is a kind of antidote to all the boringly overblown commercialised nudes one sees around now.'

As Robert took hold of her arm while they crossed Piccadilly, she went on, 'I wish you had been at the view, darling. It was terribly interesting to watch other people's reactions to the portrait. Rather sad in a way. You could see by their wistful expressions that quite a lot of the women were wishing they had a golden bed in their lives. Poor things, what a shame for them not to,' she added compassionately.

'You haven't a golden bed,' he said.

'I didn't mean *literally*, darling. It's the man who matters, not the bed.'

'Oh, I see what you mean,' said her husband, keeping his face straight but allowing a glimmer of amusement to appear in his dark eyes.

That evening, on the terrace at the Villa Delphini, David sat with his wife on his lap and his hand spread over her belly to feel their child moving inside her.

Liz had given up drinking spirits and wine since her pregnancy had been confirmed. It wasn't a deprivation. She was happy to do whatever was best for the baby. Even the loss of her slim waist she didn't mind. It was only for a few months and David seemed to find her no less desirable.

'My mother's determined to visit us,' she said, referring to a letter from Mrs Eugene P. Thornwell which had reached the villa that morning. 'I don't know how I can stop her.'

'Why try?' he said, with a smile. 'As far as I'm concerned, sweetie, she's welcome to stay for a short time.'

'I don't think you'll like her, David. She's the queen of snobs. It's only because I've managed to nobble a baronet that she's suddenly become so motherly. The fact that you're also a darling is merely a bonus. You could have been a prize rat, she would still have approved of you.'

'Perhaps she'll make a better job of being a grandmother than she did of being a mother,' he said mildly.

'Perhaps.' Liz rose from his knee and went to lean on the balustrade, looking down on the dusky harbour with the lights coming on under the awnings of the waterfront cafés.

'I don't mind any more that she was a disaster as a mother,' she said, looking over her shoulder to where he was sitting. 'You've made up for every bad thing which happened in my life before you. I've had more happiness in the last six months than most people have in a lifetime.'

'So have I.' David drained his wine glass and came to stand beside her. 'You were eminently worth waiting for,' he murmured, kissing her cheek.

As they stood with their arms round each other, in the deepening twilight, he repeated the words inscribed in the tower on the headland.

'*O what is more blessed than to throw cares aside, as the mind lays down its burdens and——*'

Liz remembered the end of the verse and they spoke the last words in unison.

'*——weary with labour and far journeys, we come home to our own place.*'

Harlequin Presents

Coming Next Month

1015 HIGH COUNTRY Sharron Cohen
TV critic Eleanora Martin pans Ben Kolter's comeback record, and his revenge is swift. The country singer writes a song about her that tops the country music charts and makes her embarrassingly famous.

1016 LOVE LIES SLEEPING Catherine George
When Francis Wilding is hired as an archivist, and she delves into the surprising past of Lord Harry Curthoy's aristocratic family, she doesn't for a moment suspect how drastically this past will affect her future.

1017 CASTLES IN THE AIR Rosemary Hammond
Widow Diana Hamilton is shocked when she learns that her husband, an American navy pilot, presumed dead for seven years, has been found alive. Can they possibly recapture the past?

1018 FANTASY UNLIMITED Claire Harrison
A young lawyer knows she has to resist her intense attraction to the exciting man she meets on a cruise ship because she suspects he was hired by her eccentric grandmother. Hired to seduce her....

1019 AFTER THE LOVING Carole Mortimer
Bryna knows her affair with Raff Gallagher won't last—even after six months she can see the break coming. So, believing for medical reasons that she can't have children, it is a shock to learn she is pregnant!

1020 THE WRONG MIRROR Emma Darcy
When Karen's twin, Kirsty, is dying in a middle-East accident she tells her news journalist lover about the son she bore him, whom she'd given to Karen to raise. After three years, Karen is faced with losing the son she regards as her own.

1021 SHADOWS IN THE LIMELIGHT Sandra K. Rhoades
What attraction does a small-time florist have for a Canadian political luminary? That's what she wants to know when he asks her to resurrect her past as Cat Devlin—the singer who fled the bright lights.

1022 SUNSET AT IZILWANE Yvonne Whittal
Frances can't understand her neighbor's antagonism and his discouraging attitude to her new venture in farming—her lifelong ambition. Then she discovers he wants her farm so he can extend his South African game farm.

Available in October wherever paperback books are sold, or through Harlequin Reader Service:

In the U.S.
901 Fuhrmann Blvd.
P.O. Box 1397
Buffalo, N.Y. 14240-1397

In Canada
P.O. Box 603
Fort Erie, Ontario
L2A 5X3

Take 4 books & a surprise gift FREE

SPECIAL LIMITED-TIME OFFER

Mail to   **Harlequin Reader Service®**

In the U.S.	In Canada
901 Fuhrmann Blvd.	P.O. Box 609
P.O. Box 1394	Fort Erie, Ontario
Buffalo, N.Y. 14240-1394	L2A 5X3

YES!   Please send me 4 free Harlequin Romance® novels and my free surprise gift. Then send me 8 brand-new novels every month as they come off the presses. Bill me at the low price of $1.99 each*—an 11% saving off the retail price. There are no shipping, handling or other hidden costs. There is no minimum number of books I must purchase. I can always return a shipment and cancel at any time. Even if I never buy another book from Harlequin, the 4 free novels and the surprise gift are mine to keep forever.   118 BPR BP7F

*Plus 89¢ postage and handling per shipment in Canada.

Name _____ (PLEASE PRINT)

Address _____ Apt. No.

City _____ State/Prov. _____ Zip/Postal Code

This offer is limited to one order per household and not valid to present subscribers. Price is subject to change.   DOR-SUB-1D

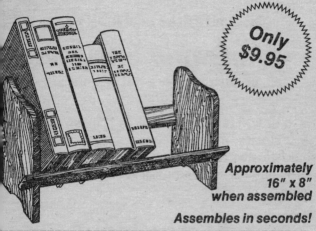

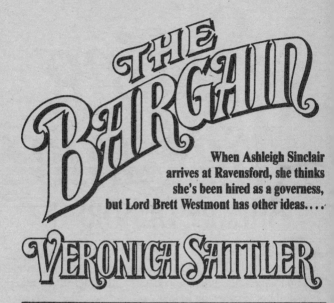